DON'T MIS

Q

QUANTUM LEAP: THE NOVEL

The thrilling debut based on the smash TV series!

TOO CLOSE FOR COMFORT

Sam's new mission could make or break the Quantum Leap Project—for ALL time.

THE WALL

What can a child do to alter the fate of Germany? Sam is about to find out.

PRELUDE

Sam's first Leap—here's how it all began . . .

KNIGHTS OF THE MORNINGSTAR

After his latest Leap, Sam finds himself wielding a sword—and facing a man in full armor!

SEARCH AND RESCUE

Sam races against time and a deadly blizzard to rescue survivors of a plane crash—including Al.

Continued . . .

RANDOM MEASURES

Al must make the ultimate choice—save Sam, or a wife he never knew he had . . .

PULITZER

Is Al a traitor to his country? Only Sam can find out for sure . . .

DOUBLE OR NOTHING

Sam leaps into two people—twin brothers who are mortal enemies . . .

ODYSSEY

Sam and Al must save a twelve-year-old from an uncertain future—and himself . . .

ANGELS UNAWARE

When Sam leaps into a priest, Al joins him as an angel in a quest to ease a woman's pain.

OBSESSIONS

A woman claiming to be Sam's wife threatens to turn Project Quantum Leap into a tabloid headline.

*And now, the latest **Quantum Leap** adventure . . .*
LOCH NESS LEAP

QUANTUM LEAP

OUT OF TIME. OUT OF BODY.
OUT OF CONTROL.

QUANTUM LEAP

LOCH NESS LEAP

A NOVEL BY

Sandy Schofield

BASED ON THE UNIVERSAL TELEVISION SERIES *QUANTUM LEAP* CREATED BY DONALD P. BELLISARIO

BOULEVARD BOOKS, NEW YORK

Quantum Leap: Loch Ness Leap, a novel by Sandy Schofield, based on the Universal television series QUANTUM LEAP, created by Donald P. Bellisario.

QUANTUM LEAP: LOCH NESS LEAP

A Boulevard Book / published by arrangement with MCA Publishing Rights, a Division of Universal Studios, Inc.

PRINTING HISTORY
Boulevard edition/July 1997

Cover art by Stephen Gardner.

The Putnam Berkley World Wide Web site address is
http://www.berkley.com

Make sure to check out *PB Plug*, the science fiction/fantasy newsletter, at
http://www.pbplug.com

ISBN: 1-57297-231-9

BOULEVARD
Boulevard Books are published by The Berkley Publishing Group, 200 Madison Avenue, New York, New York 10016.
BOULEVARD and its logo are trademarks belonging to Berkley Publishing Corporation.

PRINTED IN THE UNITED STATES OF AMERICA

10 9 8 7 6 5 4 3 2 1

To the memory of Thorne B.

Acknowledgments

Thanks on this one go to Ginjer Buchanan for waiting all these months and for being such a gem to work with; to Merrilee Heifitz for shaking her head and going with this; to Nina Kiriki Hoffman for all those nights of pizza and Leap; to Jerry and Kathy Oltion for scouting locations and for the photos; to Donald Bellisario, Deborah Pratt, Dean Stockwell, and Scott Bakula for putting on a show entertaining, thought-provoking, and heartfelt.

CHAPTER ONE

Hame, hame, hame, hame fain wad I be
O, hame, hame, hame, to my ain countrie!
—ALLAN CUNNINGHAM

Chill rain hard on his face.

The whistle of the wind, the smell of water—not rain—damp and dank and overwhelming.

His mouth tasted of peppermints, and his legs were cramped from bending at an awkward angle. The world was moving, bobbing, spinning, and he felt vaguely dizzy—not him, really. The person he'd Leaped into.

He opened his eyes and they immediately filled with water. Rain, slanted with the wind, pummeled his face. He was on a lake in a small boat, and the water was choppy.

The shore was far away.

And the man across from him was using oars instead of the motor on the back.

Sam wiped his eyes, but couldn't seem to clear them. The rain was coming down too hard. He was wearing a gray slicker and boots a size too large. The bottom of the boat was filled with two inches of water, and the man across from him was cursing.

"Use the motor!" Sam shouted.

"Did ye na hear me?" the man shouted back, his voice thin in the wind. He was squat, his arms beefy, and his face round. His features were blunted by weather. He looked like a wood carving of a sailor that Sam had seen on the California coast. " 'Tis na more."

The man's accent was thick and Gaelic, but Sam's brain was too addled to know if it was Irish or Scottish. He couldn't quite parse out what " 'Tis na more" meant either, whether it meant the engine was dead or the gas was gone.

"Put yer camera away, sir. We'll na be seeing anathing taday. I need yer back and yer good strong arms." Then the man kicked another set of oars in the boat's bottom toward Sam.

The boat was a small craft with double oarlocks and an engine on the back as an afterthought. The waves were buffeting it, and they were too much for one man. Sam bent down and a camera hit the bench between him and the other man.

"Ach, careful now," the man said. "Ye'd na wanta lose them photos of briny sticks."

Sam sensed the derision but ignored it. The camera was large, heavy, and square, with a telephoto lens. It looked like something he would have used sometime in the eighties, before cameras got lightweight and high-tech. Wrapped in plastic, it was the only thing dry against the rain.

He whipped it around his back, wincing as its weight hit his spine, and grabbed the oars. They were wet and slick, the wood slimy. He wasn't wearing gloves and the hands he saw reflected in the puddle at the bottom of the boat—big, wrinkled, male hands—didn't seem used to physical labor.

"Ye ever dun this before?"

"Yes," Sam said, although he wasn't sure when. He stuck the oars in the oarlocks, took a deep breath, and matched the other man's strokes.

The boat moved forward, cutting through the waves. A splinter dug into Sam's right index finger, and he was quickly winded despite the minimal exertion. He felt some bleed-through between his body and the body he had Leaped into. This happened on only a few Leaps, often when health was at stake. He hoped he wouldn't give whomever owned this body a heart attack. Clearly the man had not been taking care of it. No one should be this out of shape—three strokes with an oar and Sam was breathing as if he had run a marathon.

Gray hills rose behind the other man. The lake appeared to be a mile across, and extended as far as he could see in length. Few buildings graced the shore, but he didn't dare turn around to see what was behind him, to see where they were heading. This body was already in a precarious situation. He didn't want to push it too far.

The rain was sharp as needles and covered everything in a haze. Still, he could see far enough to realize that the hills were barren and the rock unfamiliar. This didn't look like any part of the States he had been to. Those hills looked *old*, like the hills he had seen in Europe when he and—

He and—

His brain stuttered. He hated that. The Swiss-cheesed memory struck again. He wasn't even sure where he had Leaped from, who he had just been. All he knew was that he was here now, in a gray slicker, in a storm, on a lake he'd never seen before. Blisters were rising on his palms, his arms ached, and each breath burned.

"Almost there, Professor," the man said. He was doing the bulk of the work.

Sweat mingled with the rain. Sam pulled on the oars, but his arms were getting so tired that they shook. Waves slapped the sides of the boat and spilled in, pouring over his large boots. His feet were wet and cold, his thick socks fat pools of ice.

"Slow down!" the man yelled.

The oars slipped from Sam's fingers, and the boat slammed against something hard and immobile, sending shivers through the wooden frame. Voices resounded behind him, and hands gripped the boat's bow.

"Jeez, Dad, the camera," a male voice said behind him.

Sam grabbed the cord and swung the camera back around. His hands hurt.

The boat had hit a dock. The other man was standing up, tossing a rope to someone behind Sam. "Tie it up good, now, lass. I'll be there inna heartbeat ta help ya."

Sam sat hunched, breathing hard. Some Leaps began better than others. He didn't like how this one started. The bleed-through presaged something bad.

"You okay, Dad?" The male voice was American and young.

The other man wasn't answering. Sam made himself breathe easier. He had to be Dad.

"I'm fine," he said. "I'm just fine."

"The professor here had ta get his hands dirty,"

the other man said. He leapt from the boat onto the dock, then pulled the boat toward shore. "This'll be a bad 'un. We're na goin' out agin till it's over."

"Aye, captain!" the young man said with a bit of a smile in his voice. Then he bent down beside Sam. He was older than Sam had expected, a man in his twenties, with sharp blue eyes and a hawk nose. His hair color was hard to tell; it looked dark because it was wet and plastered to the side of his face. It was longer than his ears, and brushed his collar in the back. "Dad?"

Sam nodded, and extended a hand, wincing at the pain in his muscles. He needed some water and some vitamins, or the muscles would be cramping soon. The young man placed a hand beneath Sam's upper arm and pulled him up onto the dock.

The wooden dock creaked beneath their weight. A girl stood to the side, well-covered in a slicker, her age indeterminate. She had wrapped the end of the rope around a post on the side of the dock. The older man had pulled the boat forward, then he nodded at her.

"Ye can untie her, Dixie, lass. I'll do it from here."

She bent over the post, working hard, her fingers slim and red from the rain, until the rope came loose. The old man pulled the boat into the back door of an ancient, weather-grayed boat shed. He closed the door behind himself.

The young man took the camera off Sam's neck. "I guess you didn't get it wet after all," he said.

"No," Sam said, "but look at it closely. It banged against the seat, and I'm afraid I might have cracked a lens."

"That won't hurt the film, though," the young man said.

The girl came over beside them. "It's my momma's camera, Travis," she said, her voice soft and young, with a pronounced Southern drawl. "She ain't gonna like it."

"She isn't here," the young man said. He leaned toward Sam. "We were watching from shore. It looked like something was out there. Did you get pictures?"

"Check the roll," Sam said, hoping his "son" knew where the counter had been before this trip started.

The young man peered at the camera through the bag. The girl leaned against him. She seemed more interested in whether or not the camera had been damaged.

"Looks like you took a few photos." The young man grinned. He had a lopsided smile that made him seem less intense, more vulnerable, and transformed his face from awkward planes and lines into something almost handsome. "So, did you see her, Dad?"

Sam glanced around, hoping for Al. The rain was coming down straight now, and the drops were thicker. The clouds to the northeast seemed even heavier than they had been a moment ago.

"I need to get inside," he said, hoping there was an inside.

"Sure," the young man said. "I should have gone out today. You're not used to that kind of exercise."

"I didn't expect to do any," Sam said.

"They said when we hired out the boat that the engine was unreliable. But this is the best place for sightings."

"There was a sightin' here in seventy-two," the girl said, as if she were repeating gospel.

Sam grunted, not sure what the proper response would be. He walked to the end of the dock, the young man and the girl a few steps behind him. *Travis and . . . Dixie?* he thought. Better get used to thinking of them by name.

"You took pictures, Dad," Travis was saying. "That means you saw something. Right?"

Sam didn't answer. The wooden dock led to a stone path that looked older than the hills across the lake. The stone wound around a rock garden, where greenery and rocks blended to provide some color against the gray sky.

But he wasn't looking at the garden. He was looking at the building in front of him. The middle section was stone so ancient that the mortar was crumbling in some places. Additions, also old, were built along its side. The roof was wood, although he suspected it had once been thatch.

"Dad? Everything all right?" Travis asked.

Sam didn't answer him. He was staring at the sign.

"He looks like a ghost done walked on his grave," Dixie was saying behind him. But Sam didn't speak to her either.

He couldn't take his attention from the sign hanging above the door. It was written in Gaelic, handcarved into wood and faded. Sam was familiar enough with Gaelic that he would have been able to parse out the meaning. But he didn't need to. The sign was translated into English and mounted on a modern plaque near the door knocker.

LOCH NESS INN
[ESTABLISHED 1620]

Loch Ness.

So, did you see her, Dad?

Now he didn't have to ask who "she" was. Or why he was looking for her. Or even why the camera was important.

He knew.

He was in Loch Ness, looking for the monster.

Sam closed his eyes.

"Oh, boy," he whispered.

CHAPTER TWO

Consciousness is a singular of which the plural is unknown, and what seems to be a plurality is merely a series of different aspects of this one thing. . . .

—ERWIN SCHRÖDINGER

Stallion's Gate, New Mexico, Now.

Samantha Josephine Fuller clutched a clipboard to her chest. The metal top dug into the soft flesh above her lab coat. She stood a half step behind Verbena Beeks, Project Quantum Leap's psychiatrist. They were just inside the door of the Waiting Room, staring at the sleeping man on the bed. They knew the Leap had happened; they knew someone new resided in Dr. Beckett's body. They just didn't know who.

Yet.

The Waiting Room always made Samantha shudder a little—she never knew what to expect from the person on the bed. But Dr. Beeks had given her permission to study the wake-up interview of each of the people who Leaped into Sam Beckett's body. Samantha's research was coming along well, and she felt that something in those wake-up interviews might give her a clue to what they were missing in the transferal process, something that might allow them to bring Dr. Beckett home.

Still, it meant she had to go into the Waiting Room. She always found its starkness startling, even though she knew it was necessary. The blue was supposed to comfort the waking traveler. The bed, little more than a cot, was supposed to be a familiar, safe haven. The temperature was a constant seventy-two degrees, warm enough to allow the visitor to remain barefoot. The chairs—when they were allowed—were wood, so as not to jolt visitors from their time periods.

Keeping people in their time periods was a top priority. In fact, Samantha had to leave her watch outside and remove most of her jewelry. Like Dr. Beeks, she wore a white lab coat, and she wasn't supposed to use any slang when she spoke—which turned out to be harder than it had originally sounded. She even took pains to hide the remains of her Southern accent, which the university had mostly beat out of her more than ten years before. Dr. Beeks had said that even an accent could make people ask questions, although in Samantha's experience, most of the people with whom Dr. Beckett traded places didn't have a lot of questions about where they were. They assumed they were in a hospital, or having a dream. But a handful had been trouble.

Especially Leon Styles, who had actually escaped and gotten off the Project grounds and into Albuquerque. Fortunately Admiral Calavicci had found him and brought him back to the Project.

They had beefed up security since then, but that didn't stop Samantha from being nervous. She never knew what to expect.

Dr. Beeks turned and gestured for Samantha to come forward. Samantha stepped beside Dr. Beeks and looked down at the man on the bed.

He looked like Dr. Beckett. That always startled her. While he slept, she could imagine that Dr. Beckett was back here, that he was about to get up and tell them how to continue the Project. But once the eyes were open, the new personality shone through, and it would become clear that Dr. Beckett was still gone.

"Coming around," Dr. Beeks said softly.

This moment always made Samantha tense. She had witnessed it several times and each time it was different. Each time gave her more—and less—information.

Dr. Beckett's body stirred. His right hand moved to his forehead, then his eyelashes fluttered. Samantha could feel a new presence in the room. One moment the room had felt normal; a second later someone else had joined them. If she could bottle that feeling, that moment, she might be able to find some of the answers she was looking for.

It had something to do with consciousness. When the body had been unconscious, she couldn't feel it.

The eyes blinked open, then the right hand hid them. Dr. Beeks straightened just a little, obviously preparing herself. Samantha suppressed a sigh. One of these times, she would like to figure out how that presence made itself felt even before the eyes opened.

Dr. Beckett's body groaned. Then the head shook slightly, as if trying to clear. Some of the visitors found the arrival painful, others simply disorienting, and a few likened it to a hangover from a long, and particularly drawn-out drunk. This one seemed painful. The visitor must have come from a long way.

The body rose on one elbow and then glanced up. The expression wasn't one of Dr. Beckett's, but it was familiar. Samantha felt a shiver run down her spine. She had seen that look before. Then his gaze fell on Dr. Beeks.

"The boat?" the visitor asked. "The storm? Is Angus all right?"

This was where the difficulties began. They had to be careful which questions they answered, particularly this early in the Leap. Ziggy, the hybrid computer at the heart of Project Quantum Leap, hadn't yet communicated to them where Dr. Beckett was, who he was, or what he was doing. If they gave the wrong answers, it would lead to confusion when the visitor returned to his or her own time.

"I need to ask you a few questions," Dr. Beeks said. Her voice was soft, nonthreatening, calm.

The visitor pushed himself completely upright, his concentration on Dr. Beeks. The newcomer had good mental abilities, Samantha noted. He—she assumed the visitor was male because he wasn't startled at the depth of Dr. Beckett's voice—had already taken control of his emotions, his questions, and his terror, and had been able to focus on Dr. Beeks. Very few new arrivals were able to do that.

"Questions," he said, and his tone was dry. "This is a hospital, isn't it?"

"I'm Dr. Verbena Beeks," she said. She took one of the chairs near the wall and pulled it over. "Some of these questions may sound strange. I'm going to ask them so that we know how well oriented you are."

The procedure was slightly new. It was a way both

to get the information Samantha needed and to help Admiral Calavicci when he finally contacted Dr. Beckett. Sometimes people in the Waiting Room couldn't answer questions. They were fortunate that this person could.

Samantha remained standing, unintroduced. She felt awkward, but she didn't grab a chair. She had decided early on in this new procedure not to call attention to herself. When Dr. Beeks was ready to introduce Samantha, she would.

"Orient myself," the newcomer repeated.

Dr. Beeks nodded. She set her own clipboard across her knee and pulled a pen from the pocket of her lab coat. "Now then," she said, "tell me the year."

The man frowned, taken aback. "Do I have a head injury?" he asked.

"Let me ask the questions," Dr. Beeks said in her firm, no-nonsense way. "Then you'll have your turn."

The newcomer glanced at Samantha as if for reassurance. His mouth dropped open. He stood, wobbled and lost his balance. Dr. Beeks rose quickly, grabbed for him, and caught his arm, bringing him down slowly. Dizziness, discomfort, and loss of balance were all common with the transfer. Obviously the visitor was built differently than Dr. Beckett.

But the man hadn't taken his gaze from Samantha's face. He shook off Dr. Beeks and tried to stand again. His feet slipped out from under him, and he caught himself on the bed.

"Sit down," Dr. Beeks said. "You shouldn't be moving like this—"

He ignored her. He was staring at Samantha. His

gaze had never left her. "Where's Travis?" he asked.

Be prepared for anything, Dr. Beeks had told her. *Be prepared.*

Samantha took a deep breath, trying to formulate an answer. The man shoved away from the bed. Dr. Beckett was a big man, and the staff kept his body in good shape. She had never been uncomfortable with that before.

"Where's Travis?" he asked again.

She shook her head, not knowing what else to do. He staggered forward a step, then looked down at his body. He raised his hands slowly, looking at the backs. Then he turned them and frowned at the palms. He plucked at the white smock, peered at his chest, then shoved the sleeves up, first one and then the other.

"What's going on here?" he asked. This time, his voice had a tinge of panic. "What's going on?"

Dr. Beeks took a hypojet from one of her lab coat pockets. Samantha didn't move.

The visitor raised his head, eyes wide. He held out his hands. "These aren't mine," he said. He looked down at his feet. They were bare, and long. "What is this place?"

Dr. Beeks removed the cap from the end of the hypo.

"Why aren't you answering me? What's happening?"

Dr. Beeks stood and pressed the hypo firmly into the newcomer's backside. Samantha heard a faint hiss as it discharged. "Sorry," she said.

He glanced at her, stunned, then collapsed. Dr. Beeks caught him. She staggered under his weight, even though she had done this dozens of times before.

Samantha hurried forward to help. She caught the man's upper arms. His eyes were slightly open, the whites showing. His head was tilted back, flopping heavily.

Together she and Dr. Beeks dragged him to the bed. They rested his torso on it, then Samantha went to his feet, lifted them, and tucked him in. Despite the heat in the room, the feet were cold.

Dr. Beeks put her hands on her hips and shook her head. "After such a promising start."

"He realized what was going on awfully fast."

Dr. Beeks nodded. "Quite a brain in there," she said. She sighed and picked up her clipboard. "You certainly caught his attention."

"I'm not sure he knew I was here until that moment," Samantha said.

"Maybe," Dr. Beeks said. She picked up her pen and put it back in her pocket. Her hands were shaking. "I don't like how this one is starting. I hope Admiral Calavicci is having more luck than we are."

Samantha glanced at the prone figure on the bed. Travis, he'd asked about . . . and that intense look. And such controlled panic. Was that how she would be in his situation? Controlled panic?

"Are you all right, Dr. Fuller?" Dr. Beeks asked.

Samantha nodded. "I'm just a bit shaken," she said, pulling the chair back and heading toward the door. "That's all."

The man's reaction had alarmed her. That, and the Waiting Room itself. Nothing more.

Except that intense look.

And the name Travis.

CHAPTER THREE

Let us not underrate the value of a fact;
it will one day flower in a truth.

—HENRY DAVID THOREAU

Loch Ness, March 14, 1986.

A fire burned inside the inn, a real fire, not the fake gas flames that Sam had seen in so many other buildings. This one filled the room with the smoky scent of unidentifiable wood. The fireplace was ancient, as old as the main building itself. The interior had been burned black, and probably hadn't been cleaned in a century. The outside stones also had charred and it was impossible to determine their original color.

The stone pattern continued across the floor. It was made of flat stone tiles across the raised area in front of the fireplace. Then, down a step, it became wood strips, strips that time and weather had put at different angles. Walking across the floor was a bit like rolling on a choppy sea.

The main room, which was probably called the public room, was wide and large, and did in fact serve as a pub. Scarred wooden tables, square and hand-built, were scattered across the floor. Mismatched chairs were pushed up to the tables, and stools stood along the bar, which ran the length of one wall. Beneath the smoky scent was another, more ancient smell, a smell of all the meals eaten in the room, and all the ale drunk. It was a reassuring, homey smell.

Despite the fire and the warmth, the room was empty.

Sam removed his hat and rain slicker and hung them on pegs near the door. Travis came in behind him and shook the water from his hair like a dog. The girl stood back, as if she had expected it.

"I don't know how people live here year round," Travis said. "We've been here two weeks and it's rained nearly every day."

"Not a storm like this one, though," Sam said, keeping his tone neutral so the phrase could function as either a question or a statement.

"No," Travis said. "Not a storm like this one."

A loud, pneumatic *whoosh!* echoed in the room, but the young man didn't turn. No one heard it except Sam. He let out a small sigh of relief.

Al was here.

Sam was about to tell the couple that he needed to be alone, when Travis said, "Shoot, Dad. Where's the camera?"

"I gave it to you," Sam said. "Did you set it down?"

"I helped you get it out of the boat." Travis turned to the girl. "You got it, Dixie?"

"You were holdin' it," she said. Her accent was one of the broadest Sam had ever heard.

"The wind's really whipping out there," Sam said.

"Don't remind me." The young man grabbed his

slicker and hat. He paused at the door. "You coming, Dixie?"

She shrugged. "Guess I'm wet enough. Why not? They say there's ghosts in the gray."

Together the two of them disappeared out the door. Sam turned around and saw the welcome face of Al. He was looking after the couple with a bemused expression.

" 'Ghosts in the gray'?" Al asked, obviously not expecting an answer. He was wearing a neon blue suit of some sort of shimmery material Sam couldn't identify. Al's boots were white, and he wore a matching white belt. He held the handlink in his right hand, a cigar in his left.

"Don't tell me," Sam said. "Disco is back in."

"It's retro," Al said. "They didn't have neon blue silk in the seventies."

"Fortunately," Sam said. He pulled up a chair. He was exhausted. His back and shoulders ached.

"What happened to you?" Al asked.

"Don't ask," Sam said. "Just tell me I'm not here to find the Loch Ness monster."

"All right," Al said. "I won't tell you."

Sam groaned and covered his face with his blistered hand.

"But that is part of it," Al said.

Sam shook his head. He knew it. He knew it the moment he had seen the sign. "Al, I don't believe a prehistoric monster can live in a lake that's only a mile wide."

"And 754 feet deep," Al said. "If such a creature exists, it can survive in this lake."

"I thought someone debunked this whole Loch Ness thing."

"Several times," Al said. "And in 1992, the guy who took the famous photograph made a deathbed confession, saying he had faked it. Of course, in the summer of 1996, a whole bunch of people saw the monster at the same time."

"Al—"

"But that's not important," Al said. "Because this is March of 1986."

"1986," Sam repeated. "March what?"

"March fourteenth. Nearly the Ides." Al grinned.

Beware the Ides of March. Sometimes, Sam thought, his classical education was not reassuring.

"You're Donald Harding, a fifty-year-old—"

"Theoretical physics professor from Stanford," Sam said. He let his hand drop. Al was staring at him in wonder.

"You know this guy?"

Sam nodded. "I don't know him, but I know of him. His work on string theory was one of the cornerstones of Project Starbright."

"Sometimes your Swiss-cheesed brain amazes me," Al said. He clutched his handlink, put the cigar in his mouth, and punched a few buttons. The handlink squealed. He puffed once, then took the cigar out of his mouth and tapped ash. It fell, then disappeared before it hit the floor. "This Leap makes Ziggy nervous, but she won't say why. Maybe that's it."

"The connection to Project Starbright?"

"Yeah. Without it, there would have been no Project Quantum Leap." Al was talking more to himself than to Sam.

"I don't think there'd be a connection," Sam said. "Dr. Harding published his theories in 1982, and I studied them that year. He expanded on them later, but most of what I used was from the earlier monograph."

"And you're sure you've never met him?" Al asked.

"Positive," Sam said, and then shrugged. "Well, as positive as I can be."

Al nodded, distracted, still looking at the handlink. He clearly didn't believe Sam. But Sam knew that he'd never met Harding. He remembered with a clarity he didn't usually have how disappointed he'd been when Harding died, disappointed that they'd never met.

Sam's heart pounded. Maybe he was supposed to prevent Harding's death. "What does Ziggy say I'm here for?"

Al hit the handlink. It flashed blue and yellow, and then squealed again. "She doesn't know."

"She doesn't—?"

"Well, she says there's a fifty percent chance that you're here to repair Harding's relationship with his son, Travis."

"The guy who just went after the camera."

Al nodded, then frowned at the door. "Apparently Harding and his son had a major falling out here in Loch Ness and never spoke to each other again. Harding abandoned physics research, spent his remaining years teaching, and died six years later, alone."

"Let me guess," Sam said, making a circle with his out-of-shape arm. "Heart attack."

Al glanced at the handlink, then shook his head. "Suicide."

Sam let out a sigh of air, then pushed himself away from the table. He stood and paced. "Suicide." So many of his colleagues, researchers mostly, had lonely lives, living only for whatever projects they were involved in.

Like him, in some ways. Never going home, too consumed in work to move beyond it. Only his colleagues had the choice to go home.

He didn't.

"And Ziggy thinks this estrangement from his son did it?"

"Yeah." Al brought the handlink down. "Harding's wife died in childbirth, and he never remarried. He brought Travis up on his own. But the kid's a rebel. He refused to study science and took up with the Ghostbuster crowd at Stanford in the early seventies, volunteering to be one of their guinea pigs."

"The Ghostbuster crowd?" Sam said.

"The paranormal wackos," Al said.

"I thought you believed in that sort of thing."

"Not when they're getting government dollars to see if someone can sense an ace of diamonds a room away," Al said. "Vegas should be sponsoring that research, not the U.S. government. Takes money away from real projects."

"Like Quantum Leap?"

"You got it," Al said, punctuating the words with his cigar. They had to be in the middle of a new fiscal year, Sam guessed, which always meant, for Al, a new fiscal crisis.

"He couldn't have been very old," Sam said.

"He started in seventy-two, when he was twelve. By the time Dad caught on, young Travis was a true believer in everything from UFOs to poltergeists to spoon-bending."

Sam frowned at Al's mention of UFOs. He seemed

to remember a light in the woods, blurry—and then nothing. "We've encountered a few unexplainable things, Al," Sam said. "We don't even know what's Leaping me through time."

"In every profession, there's legitimate folks and then there's wackos," Al said. "Travis has a love of the wackos. By the time his dad dies, Travis is a famous psychic with his own hotline."

"A hotline?" Sam said. "Like a drug crisis line?"

"Yeah," Al said. "Only this hotline is designed to separate the gullible from their money. Young Travis here makes a fortune, but didn't have the psychic awareness to know his dad was about to bite it. Apparently, Travis's infomercial was running on the channel that Donald Harding's TV was tuned to when he committed suicide."

"But that's years away," Sam said. "Why does Ziggy think there's a connection to now?"

"Because *this* trip is the last time the two of them spoke."

Sam stopped at the bar. There was a window to his left, a window so old the glass had been hand-blown. It had bubbles. Through its scratched, wavy surface, he saw Travis on the dock, clutching his hat in the wind. He waved to Dixie, who then disappeared into the boathouse.

"I still don't understand," Sam said. "When I Leaped into Dr. Harding, he was out on Loch Ness, with a camera around his neck."

"Travis has been fascinated with the Loch Ness monster since he was a little boy," Al said. "He wants to put together an expedition to search for the monster using sonar."

"I thought that had already been tried by 1986," Sam said.

"Several times," Al said, "but not like this. Travis wants to put two dozen boats side by side across the lake, have them drop a deep-scan sonar curtain, and then sweep the lake back and forth until they find something."

"Sounds expensive," Sam said.

"But if something's there, they'd find it," Al said. "The problem is that Travis wants Dr. Harding to fund his participation and to help with the fund-raising for the rest of it."

"That's what we're doing here?" Sam asked, surprised. He couldn't believe a man so opposed to his son's studies would go so far as to even be in Scotland.

"Dr. Harding wouldn't fund Travis unless he felt the expedition had merit." Al answered. "So that's what they're doing here. Dr. Harding is studying the evidence for himself, trolling the lake, and trying to determine if the expedition is a good idea."

"In the original history, he decided against it," Sam said.

"That's right," Al said.

Through the window, Sam saw Travis pick up the camera, examine it, then sling it around his neck. "So all I need to do is agree to the expedition, and I can Leap."

"It's not that easy, Sam," Al said. "This expedition would cost a great deal of money. Dr. Harding's reputation would be on the line, not Travis's. And you know what happens to a scientist who becomes mixed up in the paranormal. His perfect credentials get tainted."

Sam knew that all too well. He'd seen too many colleagues lose positions, lose prestige, lose all that they had built by espousing the wrong opinion.

"So if I repair Donald Harding's relationship with his son, I ruin his reputation."

Al nodded. "That's right, Sam."

Sam pulled away from the window. The room seemed dark despite the fact that it was the middle of the day. "Something bothers me, Al. Fifty percent—"

At that moment the door opened and Travis stepped in, stomping his feet and shaking the water from his coat. He held the camera in his hands.

"It was still on the dock," he said.

The handlink squealed. Al squinted at it, hit it, then squinted at it again. "I'll be right back, Sam," he said. The holographic door whooshed open behind him, filling the room with blue light. He disappeared into the light, and the door closed with its normal bang.

Sam blinked in the sudden darkness.

"Did you hear me, Dad? We were lucky it didn't fall in."

"Yes," Sam said. He was still a bit disoriented by what Al had told him. Donald Harding's suicide seemed important, but Sam didn't understand how it followed from these events. Something further in the future must have triggered him. And this fifty percent chance that Ziggy gave seemed slight. Sam had the sense something else was going on here, something besides an ideological debate.

Al had said Ziggy was bothered by this Leap. Harding's future suicide wouldn't have that effect, would it? Had Sam used more of Harding's research than he remembered? Had Harding done some additional work that Sam relied on, work that Harding developed right around this time?

March 14, 1986 didn't mean much to Sam as a date, but then, with all the holes in his memory, he wasn't sure if his feeling was accurate.

"Dad? Are you all right?" Travis was beside him now, smelling of rain and wet cloth.

"Fine," Sam said. "Where's Dixie?"

"She went to help Angus with something." Travis frowned. "You sure you're all right? You don't look that good."

"Just tired myself out rowing. I'm not used to that."

"You didn't have to go without me," Travis said. He walked to the fire, set the camera on a nearby table, and unwrapped the plastic. "In fact, I would have preferred that you waited for me."

Sam approached him, uncertain what to do. He felt as if he had stepped into the middle of an argument, an argument that had been going on for years.

"Is the camera all right?" he asked.

"What do you care?" Travis said. His fingers got caught in the wet plastic. He shook it off, and it fell to the floor. "You know, for all the money we're spending, we could have put a real research mission together. Going out and hoping to photograph something is amateur stuff."

"We agreed—"

"You agreed! Dixie and I came along for the ride, hoping you'd believe we have a case here. But you made up your mind before you came. This stuff is myth, legend, hogwash. It's not real."

Sam picked up the wet plastic. "I thought that's

what you're trying to prove, whether or not the monster's real."

"I can't prove it with a single camera and a father who thinks I'm nuts!"

"I don't," Sam said. He took a deep breath. How to tackle this topic? He had to. If Al was right, this was the center of the fight between Travis and his father. Maybe it wasn't all black and white, relationship versus reputation. Maybe Sam could find a compromise. "I just have a different way of looking at the world. A scientist quantifies things. Until we can measure something, it doesn't exist."

"That's not true, and you know it. Your whole area of research is based on quads or whatever," Travis said, "Things that don't exist."

"Quarks," Sam said, thankful he was familiar with Harding's research. "And they do exist. We just haven't seen them yet."

"Well, that's the same with the monster. It does exist. And unlike quads or quarks or whatever they are, people have seen it. People have filmed it. There are more than three thousand sightings. That's evidence, Dad."

"That's anecdote, Travis," Sam said, keeping his voice calm. "No one can prove the photographs are real. Some of the best minds have worked on quarks—"

"Some of the best minds?" Travis said. "As if no good minds have worked on the monster? Is it so hard to believe in a particle that is so small it can't be seen or measured *and* a creature so large that it looks like an ancient sea serpent? What's the stretch here? I don't see any, except that one is labeled science while the other is labeled crackpot." He swept up the camera and put it around his neck. ''I don't know why I even brought you here. You'll never open your mind to this stuff. If something doesn't fit into your narrow beliefs, it doesn't exist. I learned that as a kid. It's amazing that I have to constantly relearn it as an adult.''

He shoved chairs aside as he crossed the room. They fell, clattering on the wooden floor.

''Wait, Travis,'' Sam said.

But Travis didn't stop. When he reached the side door he slammed through it. By the time Sam stepped over all the fallen chairs, Travis was gone.

CHAPTER FOUR

We say that inseparable quantum interconnectedness of the whole universe is the fundamental reality, and that relatively independently behaving parts are merely particular and contingent forms within this whole.

—DAVID BOHM

Stallion's Gate, New Mexico, Now.

Al stepped out of the Imaging Chamber, still clutching the handlink. He felt vaguely dizzy. It wasn't physical, it was purely mental. He knew he was still at the Project, but it felt as if he were somewhere else—in this case, beside Loch Ness in Scotland.

The inn's common room had been rustic and looked older than the United States. It had seemed, in that dark homey space, as if Sam had Leaped not to 1986, but to 1786. Fortunately there were no Beckett relatives in Scotland at that time—at least, Al hoped not. It was possible, he supposed, since the Beckett name was definitely British. Al shook the thought from his head. The Leap that had sent Sam back to the American Civil War had been bad enough.

Leaping across time and space to eighteenth-century Scotland would be even worse.

Still, something was bothering Ziggy, and it had nothing to do with Donald Harding's relationship to his son Travis. There was an anomaly on this Leap, and Ziggy wasn't telling him what it was. That worried Al. If he didn't know, Sam wouldn't know. And that might mean that Sam would tamper with something he shouldn't.

The thought terrified Al. The whole thing terrified Al, if he allowed it. He had nightmares sometimes that he couldn't find Sam anywhere, that he spent days in the Imaging Chamber, searching decade after decade, arriving when Sam had left, or catching glimpses of him Leaping to a new destination. Al rarely let these fears surface, but sometimes they did, when a Leap felt different, felt wrong.

This one felt disastrous, and Al couldn't say why.

He stood outside the door to the Imaging Chamber, clutching the handlink like a lifesaver. The main room seemed the same, dominated by the multicolored high-tech machine that was Ziggy's external shell. Gooshie stood beside the console, his familiar square face creased with worry. Tina stood behind him, wearing a skintight dress beneath her lab coat, a dress Al had heartily approved of when she'd put it on that morning.

"Al?" Tina asked.

His face must have shown his concern, something he always tried to avoid. Never, ever let 'em know you're worried.

"Ziggy," he said, stepping toward the computer. Her main console was pulsing yellow today. He hadn't quite figured out what the colors meant. Sometimes they seemed to have a pattern, and sometimes they didn't. "What gives?"

"You'll need to be more specific, Admiral," Ziggy said, her voice low and sexy. He didn't like this new voice, hadn't liked it since it first appeared. With it had come some quirks of personality that made Al decidedly uneasy.

"You and I both know Sam's not there to help Harding and his son reunite. Fifty percent are the lowest odds you've ever given. Tell me what's really going on." He stopped in front of the machine. Her lights started flashing, as if she was working extra hard. The yellow disappeared, and Ziggy ran through all the colors in the spectrum, from red to blue and back down again. The colors were playing on Gooshie's face like an insane strobe light.

"I've told you all I know, Admiral," Ziggy said.

"There've been times when she didn't even know why Dr. Beckett Leaped or what he was supposed to put right," Gooshie said, trying to placate Al.

"I beg to differ," Ziggy said. "I have always known what Dr. Beckett was supposed to put right. I have not always known what would trigger his Leap."

"That's one way to put it," Al said. He leaned on the edge of the console, which made Tina wince. "But something's going on here, and it's clearly affecting you. I need to know what it is."

"The time line is in constant flux, Admiral," Ziggy said. "It has been since Dr. Beckett arrived in 1986. I have had trouble getting a fix on his location, and on his mission, as well as on his brain wave patterns."

"You didn't seem to have any trouble getting me there," Al said.

"Actually, she did, Admiral," Gooshie said, moving forward. Al ducked back. Gooshie's lunch had been heavy on the garlic and onions. That, mixed with his normal halitosis, created one of the most powerful odors Al had ever encountered. "There was a moment when everything whirred."

"Whirred?" Al asked.

"That's pretty accurate," Tina said. "Ziggy's entire board lit up. The room was, like, psychedelic."

"What happened, Ziggy?" Al asked.

"It's hard to put in layman's terms, Admiral."

He winced, hating to be patronized by a computer, even one as brilliant as Ziggy. "Try."

The room became incredibly silent. It was almost as if Ziggy were trying to choose the right words, the way a human would. Perhaps she was. In some ways, Ziggy reminded Al of all his ex-wives rolled into one.

Particularly when she was being patronizing.

"It was as if there was a storm in the time line, Admiral," Ziggy said. "A brief, powerful storm that shook up everything from 1986 on. It only lasted for a moment, and then I was able to place you in the Loch Ness Inn."

"What caused it?" Al asked.

"I do not know. Something quite powerful."

"The monster?" Gooshie asked. Both Al and Tina looked at him. He shrugged, then slowly flushed until the color of his cheeks matched the color of his hair. "I've been a Loch Ness monster buff since I was a boy."

"Figures," Al mumbled.

"No," Ziggy said, as if their interaction hadn't occurred. "It was something more profound than that."

"More profound than a monster. Good," Al said. He shoved his cigar in his mouth. Tina frowned at him. Al took the cigar out. He could hear her admonition without her saying anything. *You don't want to get ash in Ziggy's circuits, do you*?

Yes, Tina. Sometimes he did. It might be good for the old girl.

"Did Sam somehow mess with Dr. Harding's research?"

"Admiral," Ziggy said, "Dr. Beckett already told you that Dr. Harding published the relevant research for Project Starbright four years before this Leap is taking place. Which means that Dr. Harding finished the research and checked his results years before that—"

"I know how scientific research works," Al said. He glanced at the handlink he was still clutching. He felt as if it bound him to Sam, that if he let it go, Sam would be on his own in an uncertain past.

"Then you would have known that your question wasn't logical," Ziggy said.

"Look," Al said. "Something's going screwy with this Leap. You know it, and it was pretty clear to me in that inn. We need to find it, and quickly. The last time something went screwy—"

"You and Dr. Beckett switched places," Gooshie said.

"Actually, the last time," Ziggy said, her voice somber, "Admiral Calavicci ceased to exist."

Al brought his head up. Tina's eyes widened. Ziggy kept track of all the alternate time lines. Al's stomach flipped. He wasn't certain he wanted to know *every-*

thing that went wrong. Especially if he had once "ceased to exist."

"So, uh, I guess Dr. Beckett fixed that one," Tina said.

"Clearly," Ziggy said.

Al felt alternately hot and cold. The time line had a storm in it. The last time things had gone screwy, someone from the Project had been involved.

Gooshie obviously understood where Al's mind was going. So did Tina. "I've never been to Scotland," Gooshie said.

"Me, either," Tina said.

"I have." The voice came from behind him. Al turned, but he didn't have to. He recognized the voice. It belonged to Samantha J. Fuller, Sam Beckett's daughter. Al remembered everything to do with Samantha. Sam had Leapt into the life of Samantha's mother, Abagail Fuller, three times, and in each instance he saved her life. In the third instance, he not only saved her life, but he saved his daughter's future. Samantha, whose intelligence wasn't quite as high as Sam's but was still off the Richter scale, had joined the Project instead of wasting away in some trailer park down South.

With his Swiss-cheesed brain, Sam didn't remember her. And Samantha's access to all parts of the Project were limited. She didn't know who her real father was.

Samantha was standing near the entrance, arms wrapped around a clipboard. A strand of hair slipped from her French braid. With a worried frown etched between her slender eyebrows, she was the spitting image of her mother. Dark brown hair, delicately pretty features, and a look of never-ending concern.

"I know I'm not supposed to be in here right now—" she started.

"You've been to Scotland?" Al asked.

"With my boyfriend, Travis Harding. In 1986."

"Admiral—" Gooshie said.

"Not now, Gooshie." Al swallowed. Hard. What could Sam have done that would affect Samantha and the Project? What could he have done?

"Al—"

"Admiral—"

"Admiral—"

Tina, Gooshie and Ziggy were speaking in unison. Al whirled toward them. "Just wait!" he snapped.

"I'm sorry, Admiral." Ziggy was the one who answered him. "But we seem to have a problem. I've lost contact with Dr. Beckett."

"Lost contact? But you know where he is."

"Yes, I do. But there's no way for you to reach him, Admiral. I'm no longer registering his brain pattern."

Samantha. Something had happened with Samantha. Something she would remember. "Dr. Fuller," he said, turning back toward her. And then he froze.

Samantha was gone.

CHAPTER FIVE

A spark has often kindled a big fire.
—SCOTTISH PROVERB

Sam picked up the chairs that had fallen. He did not go after Travis. He needed time to cool off, and Sam needed time to think.

He sat down in one of the chairs. It creaked beneath his weight, but felt extremely comfortable, as if it had been carved for him. The public room of this inn seemed familiar, as if he had been here before, feet outstretched before him, an ale in one hand. He could almost imagine other travelers from throughout history, steam rising off their rain-soaked clothing as they warmed up near a peat fire.

The inn was amazingly quiet, but then he didn't know what time of day it was, or even how many people were staying here. Judging from the light, it was midafternoon. Sometime soon, he'd have to figure out where his room was and how to get dinner.

And what he was really supposed to do on this Leap.

He'd felt uneasy since he'd arrived here. Some of it was the natural result of a Leap. Although he was getting used to thinking on his feet, he still wasn't comfortable with finding himself in the middle of someone else's life.

Some of the unease was caused by the discomfort the rowing had provoked in Donald Harding's body. Despite Al's assurances, Harding didn't feel healthy. He was overweight and unused to exercise. Perhaps he would have refused to row his way back or perhaps he would have found a way to conserve energy. Sam had thrown himself into the task, expecting Harding's body to react the way his own would have.

But Sam was recovering quicker than he had expected. It actually felt as if the link between the two bodies was gone. It felt like Sam was himself again. He wondered what would have caused that, what would have made him feel like Harding for a while, and then feel like himself.

And the transition had been sudden. One moment, Sam had felt exhausted, his muscles cramping. The next, it felt as if even the blisters were gone. Although the tiredness remained, it was no longer a physical tiredness. Only the mental exhaustion he had felt on the last few Leaps.

Then there was Travis. This fight between the two of them felt so old that Sam wondered if he could have any influence on it at all. Children often rebelled against their parents. While parents found it annoying, it didn't usually drive them to suicide—not even single parents like Harding.

Al's odd behavior, and Ziggy's weak prediction, made Sam even more uneasy. Something else was going on. Something he had yet to figure out.

The wind whistled outside and rain pelted the building. Sam closed his eyes for what seemed like a moment. When he opened them again, they were gummy, as if he'd slept, and his clothes felt drier. A woman stood over him, arms crossed over her chest. She wore jeans tucked into boots, and a thick cable sweater that didn't hide her thinness. In the dim light she looked familiar—

Abagail?

—and unfamiliar at the same time. She was young, her thin mouth set in a line, her gray eyes recalling eyes he had seen before, a lot, every day. . . .

He shook his head, trying to rid himself of the familiar feeling. Beneath it was something else. He was drawn to her. Not attracted, nothing sexual at all, but an empathy, a fellow feeling, a *link* of some sort.

"Are you proud a yourself?" she asked. Her voice was young, with a broad Southern accent.

Sam forced himself to sit up. He had been asleep. His back ached from the unusual position, and he had a kink in his neck. He rubbed it. "Dixie?"

"Who else would it be?" she asked.

That's why she looked so familiar. He had thought, on the dock, that she was younger. A girl, a daughter, perhaps, or a friend of one of the other guests.

"Don't look so shocked. I can talk." She put her hands on her hips. "Travis was so looking forward to this trip. He thought maybe, this time, you could work things out. He thought maybe even you'd see things his way. But you ain't even tried."

Sam didn't know how to respond. She seemed more centered at this moment. Older, yes, and more mature. He wasn't sure how he had mistaken her for a girl.

"I, um, went out on the boat," he said, not sure

what to say, wishing Al would come back so that they could consult.

"Yes, to make fun of every little thing. What was it you said at breakfast? You said, 'I think I'll go have me a monster hunt,' and you said it in that way, the way Travis hates, and I was so glad he wasn't there to hear. But you still managed to hurt him when you come back."

Maybe the feeling was left over from Harding. Maybe Harding had some sort of link with her, something Sam would learn about.

"I—I didn't mean to," Sam said.

"That's right," she said. "You never mean to. You just do. You're so supremely con-*fi*-dent, Mr. Famous Scientist, that you never care how your son feels, how maybe he thinks he can contribute in a different way. You don't think things through."

"Listen," Sam said. "This whole day has been off kilter. I—"

"And now it's worse 'coz I'm talking to you, really talking to you, is that it? Travis's mousy girlfriend, the Southern one, the one with only a high school education, the one who never says nothing—"

"I never said you were mousy—"

"The one you'd swear has a brain, if only she'd show sign of it." She tilted her head slightly and raised an eyebrow. A touch of humor. Familiar—

Abagail!

—and unfamiliar.

"Didn't think I heard that, did you?" she asked. During her tirade, she had uncrossed her arms and placed her hands on her hips. The stance looked better, as if she were more accustomed to it. "Well, I did, and I do have a brain, even if it ain't trained like yours. And I have a memory too. I know all them other things you said about me, all them things you say to Travis. No wonder he don't wanta follow in your footsteps. You're a mean, hateful, lonely man who wants everybody else in the world to be mean, hateful, and lonely too.''

Then she whirled, her hair flying around her—

Like Abagail's

—and she stalked out of the room.

He let out his breath. People were stalking out on him today, over and over. He rubbed his eyes. The mental exhaustion was gone, but in its place was a confusion so deep he wasn't even sure when he was or whom he had seen.

Abagail, warm in his arms

Abagail, pleading with him

Abagail, her skin so soft beneath his . . . .

Dixie wasn't Abagail, but she reminded him of Abagail. Abagail without the obsession. Abagail with bad grammar. Abagail with such an intelligence flowing from her eyes, an intelligence that reminded him of—

Didn't think I heard that, did you?

What had Harding said?

The one you'd swear has a brain, if only she'd show sign of it.

Not very nice. Cruel, in fact, to say of a son's girlfriend. Sam rubbed his thumb and forefinger on the bridge of his nose, fighting a sudden headache. What had he read about Harding, all those years ago?

That Harding was a brilliant researcher. That he understood theoretical physics better than most. That he was the first to tie his work on string theory to work on supersymmetry.

Nothing on him as a person.

In fact, Harding hadn't even presented his monographs. He'd never shown up at conferences.

The flicker of a memory:

Sam, thin, nervous, shy among his peers, saying to—whom? another scientist, someone he should remember—*But I wanted to meet him. His work is so important to me.*

And the scientist—a woman?—all he can remember is her smile, slightly sad, deprecating. *Trust me, Dr. Beckett. You don't want to meet him.*

Sam stood, slowly, using the table for support. Maybe Al was wrong. Maybe he misinterpreted the information. Maybe Harding wasn't the victim. Maybe he was the victimizer.

You're a mean, hateful, lonely man . . . .

And maybe she was a jealous, possessive young woman who only saw things as her boyfriend did.

But that didn't feel right. And her tie to Abagail, the link he felt, the bits of memory, made him even more willing to trust her word.

He went to the door and pulled it open. The hallway beyond was narrow and smelled damp. Water trickled down one wall. A stone staircase, worn with years of use, wound around one wall. There was no railing.

From above, he could hear voices.

". . . just go home. He's not gonna change his mind. He'll never change his mind. I don't even know why you're tryin'." Dixie.

"He's so close, honey." Travis. "He studies the right things. He works with things that have less validity than the monster. He just doesn't realize it yet."

"And what are you tryin' to prove, Travis? Even

if he wakes up tomorrow a different man, how can that help you? You don't want him to believe in the monster. You don't even care if he understands our research. You just want him to believe in you."

Silence followed. Sam's breathing sounded abnormally loud in the small space. He held his breath, and it seemed as if those above him did too.

"Believing the research is believing in me," Travis said softly.

Sam took a deep breath and leaned against a thick wooden beam. What had Harding done in the latter part of the eighties? Or in the nineties? Wasn't his research basically done after he finished his superstring theories? He didn't lecture. He kept his tenure at Stanford, but he didn't do conferences, he didn't publish anymore. His reputation was made.

It seemed simple. All Sam had to do was walk up the stairs, announce an about-face, and help Travis plan a scientific way to research the monster.

He started for the stairs then stopped, obituaries, of all things, running through his mind. Scientist after scientist, from Charles Darwin to Linus Pauling, were depicted in their obituaries as having shown promise, with their early contributions but that promise having gone awry when the scientist espoused an unpopular cause.

Monsters weren't popular. Neither were ghosts or witches or demons. Sam didn't have enough information. Maybe Dixie was wrong. Maybe she hated Harding for reasons Sam as yet didn't understand. Maybe he was going about this all wrong.

Where was Al when he needed him? Their brief contact earlier had felt strained. Sam needed to bounce ideas off him, to confirm a few theories.

But Al hadn't come back yet.

Sam was on his own.

CHAPTER SIX

> We live before and after
> And pine for what is not
> —PERCY BYSSHE SHELLEY,
> "TO A SKYLARK"

Stallion's Gate, New Mexico, Now.

"Dr. Fuller?" Gooshie asked. His voice had a querulous quality. "Admiral, are you all right?"

Al was still leaning on Ziggy. His hand was on her cool plastic surface, the sharp edges of the plane cutting into his palm. In his other hand, the handlink felt too warm, almost hot, against his skin. He swallowed, feeling the same momentary disorientation that he sometimes felt when he came out of the Imaging Chamber.

He and Gooshie were alone in the large, slightly cold room. Al blinked. They hadn't been alone a moment ago.

"Dr. Fuller," Al repeated, then cleared his throat. The obstruction was still there. His stomach was churning. "What happened to Dr. Fuller, Ziggy?"

"There is no Dr. Fuller in this time line, Admiral." Ziggy, at least, still sounded like herself. Slightly patronizing, a bit controlling. And he no longer minded.

"If she's not here, then how come I can remember her?" Al asked.

"The effect won't last long, Admiral. If you were in the Imaging Chamber, you might even remember the entire past time stream."

Al was using Ziggy's side for balance. He had lost his cigar. Not only had he lost Samantha Fuller, he had lost his cigar. He patted his pockets. He wasn't wearing the neon blue silk anymore either. His outfit was purple. Purple and black, with no pockets. No place to keep a cigar.

"All right, Ziggy," Al said, "this is important. You're gonna have to help me remember her, because obviously Sam changed something with her."

"Admiral, I can't make you do something you do not want to do."

"Dammit," Al said, slamming his hand on the console. The slap echoed, and Ziggy's frame almost seemed to shake.

"Admiral," Gooshie said, his tone reprimanding. The smell of garlic, at least, was gone. But his halitosis remained.

Al ignored him. "You'll help me, Ziggy."

"Of course, Admiral," she said, as if he hadn't spoken with ferocity, as if he had asked her to locate his cigar.

"Samantha Fuller is the center of this mission," Al said.

"Now she is." Ziggy sounded vaguely disapproving.

"You'll have to get me to Sam."

"If you'll remember, Admiral, that's the problem."

Al took a deep breath and released it, trying to calm

himself. "I thought maybe with the loss of Dr. Fuller—"

"No, Admiral," Ziggy said.

Al ran his hand down his face. Gooshie was watching him. Of course, from his point of view, Al's burst of temper had been completely inexplicable. Gooshie looked the same. The same labcoat, the same ugly brown pants, the same red hair in the same short haircut. All the same, except for the mustard stain on his left sleeve. Al could have sworn that hadn't been there before.

"Where's Tina?" Al asked.

Gooshie's eyes widened then narrowed. He knew better than to tilt his head, than to look at the Admiral as if Al were crazy. Gooshie had seen a lot of changes. But sometimes it seemed to him as if he were the only sane one on the Project.

"She's visiting her parents, Admiral, remember?" Gooshie spoke slowly, like one would speak to the very young. "She's helping her mother get settled after the accident."

"Accident?" Al asked. He wasn't liking this time line. Not at all. No Samantha Fuller, no cigar, and now, no Tina.

"The car accident. She broke her arm."

"Tina broke her arm?"

"No, her mother did," Gooshie said.

"I thought her mother was dead," Al said.

"Really," Gushie said, this time letting the shock fill his voice. "Admiral. Her mother was just here two weeks ago, visiting. Remember?"

"No, I don't remember," Al snapped. And it was probably just as well. He never liked it when the in-laws—or the nearest equivalent—visited. "Things just changed. One moment Tina's here, the next she's not. And so was—so was—" He waved the handlink in exasperation "—you know. What's her name."

"Dr. Fuller," Ziggy said.

"Right," Al said. "Dr. Fuller." He was already forgetting. And he couldn't. Because Sam had to put things back the way he had found them. They couldn't lose Dr. Whatshername now. She was too . . .

She was too . . .

Important, probably, but he could no longer remember how, or why. He sighed and put his head down on his arm. What a mess.

"I suggest, Admiral, that you wait for your nap." Ziggy again. She was going to irritate him throughout this entire Leap, he knew it. "We need to find Dr. Beckett."

"Find him?" Al raised his head. She had gotten his attention this time. "He's on Loch Ness on March 14, 1986. We didn't lose him. We just lost the hookup."

"Technically, Admiral, that is correct," Ziggy said. "But our time line has just changed. We do not know if Dr. Beckett's has too. If he has Leaped, we have no way of knowing."

"Sure we do," Al said. "We check the Waiting Room. If Donald Harding is still there, Sam's still in Loch Ness."

"Forgive me, Admiral," Ziggy said, "but it is not that simple. Dr. Beckett changed history. He might still be living Dr. Harding's life, but we no longer have any guarantee that Dr. Harding is in Loch Ness. After all, there were four people in this room only a few moments ago."

"Four?" Gooshie asked.

"Four," Al said. "You, me, Tina, and Dr. Whatshername."

"Fuller," Ziggy said. "Dr. Samantha J. Fuller."

"Right," Al said. The name tweaked him. It was familiar. But of course it was familiar. He had known her in another life. He set the handlink down. His hand had cramped and the link had left indentations in his skin.

He leaned forward. "There's something I don't get," he said. "If Sam changed the past, then how come we can't reach him now? Things have changed. Things are different. Whatever caused the block in the time line should have cleared up, right? I mean, after all, we've been doing the Project now for years, and Dr. Beckett has been Leaping all this time. If Dr. Whatshername—"

"Fuller," Ziggy and Gooshie said in unison.

"—is really gone, then the changes should have been made, and we should be able to reach Sam."

"That does seem logical," Gooshie said.

"Obviously," Ziggy said, "the changes are still continuing. Dr. Fuller was an important part of Project Quantum Leap. But she was not essential. Her true importance comes from other areas. I believe, though, that the changes have only begun. As I told you before, Admiral, Dr. Beckett has landed in the equivalent of a storm in the time line. In a few moments, everything could be different *again*. That's probably what's causing the difficulties in the contact."

Al stood up. He pondered what Ziggy said for a moment, then what he could remember from before—which was fading rapidly—and the moments with Sam in the Loch Ness Inn. "What you're telling me," he said, "is that you don't know why our link with Sam is broken."

"Most of what we deal with, Admiral, is theory based on very solid evidence," Ziggy said.

"Conjecture," Gooshie added helpfully.

"Actually," Ziggy said, "conjecture implies guesswork. I do not deal in guesswork. My responses are based on probabilities, statistics, and—"

"Conjecture," Al said firmly. He didn't like this. He didn't like any of this. He felt as if he were standing on a sandy cliff face, watching the wind blow it all away. "Our first step is to find Sam. Our second is to reestablish the link. Gooshie, I want everyone working on this. And I mean everyone. Get Tina back here. The entire staff needs to make this a full focus."

Gooshie nodded. Al straightened his suit coat and glanced down at it to see if there were any pockets he had missed. None. Had he decided to quit smoking again and forgotten? Impossible. He had sworn he would never quit when he returned from 'Nam all those years ago.

"Admiral, we might need you in the Imaging Chamber," Gooshie said.

"I know," Al said. "Call me if you do."

"Where're you going?" Gooshie asked.

"To the Waiting Room. We have a Grade A, Number One Physics Brain in there. It may not be as good as Sam's but it's close."

Gooshie's small mouth made an even smaller O of surprise.

"You're not going to tell him about the Project, are you?"

"Why not?" Al asked.

"Be-Because, when he goes back—"

''He'll go back when Sam puts things right, and he won't remember any of this.''

''But what if Dr. Beckett doesn't put things right?'' Gooshie asked.

Al gave Gooshie his sternest gaze. ''He will. He always does.''

CHAPTER SEVEN

If you are sure you understand everything that is going on, you are hopelessly confused.

—WALTER MONDALE

Mount Shasta, California, Now.

Sammi Jo Harding smeared the tomato stain on her "Give Me All Your Chocolate . . . And Nobody Gets Hurt" T-shirt and sighed. She set down the half-eaten slice next to the rest of the large pepperoni, sausage, and mushroom pizza she'd ordered and grabbed a rag. Now she would have to do laundry.

And dishes.

And unpack.

She sighed again. The house she rented in Mount Shasta City was small—a 1950s "starter" home, barely 1,000 square feet—with a kitchen, a single bedroom that had once been two tiny bedrooms, and a living room the size of a Ford sedan. Still the place seemed cavernous. She had brought a few pieces of furniture with her, lugged on the smallest U-Haul trailer attached to the back of her ancient, battered Volkswagen Rabbit. When she'd arrived, she'd spent

$20 of her dwindling bank account to buy a table (painted red with green legs), two rickety chairs, and a desk for her mammoth computer system.

The pizza sat on top of the newspapers she'd been stealing from her next-door neighbor's recycling bin. She'd been meaning to put the papers back after she read them, but she never seemed to find the time.

Just like she hadn't found the time to do the laundry.

Or clean.

Or unpack.

Divorce played such havoc with a person's mental state.

She whipped her shirt off and carried it to the sink. The house was too hot, as always. She felt better shirtless, but she also didn't dare parade around semi-nude. Someone might drop in, although it was unlikely considering that she didn't know a soul in this town.

As she put some Ivory soap on the shirt and ran cold water through the stain, she wondered if she had enough quarters for the Laundromat. The thought of breaking her last hundred-dollar bill—the last of her money in the world—made her wince.

Steve's offer was looking better and better all the time.

She hung the shirt over one of the rickety chairs in the tiny kitchen, then rummaged in a nearby box, pulling out a T-shirt. This one had "Class of '84" emblazoned across the front in the colors of her high school. Long time ago now. The shirt had a hole in the left sleeve, but it still fit. Or maybe, she should say that it fit once again.

She'd lost twenty pounds since she'd left Travis.

And it wasn't because of her diet—she'd been surviving on pizza. She had lost twenty pounds because of the stress.

Travis would laugh if he knew how short of money she was. He'd made so much fun of her and her earning potential when she'd fallen in with the Silicon Valley crowd. "Real science, huh, Dixie?" he'd said, and she hadn't realized then that in his sneer, he was transferring his anger at his father to her.

She grabbed the piece of pizza and the half-finished Diet Coke and carried them into the living room. A television stood on a box, and an armchair, part of a set she'd bought with Travis, rested a few feet away from it. A computer screen provided the room's only illumination. She kicked forward the scarred wooden chair she'd bought at a garage sale, and sat slowly, putting the pizza in her mouth and tapping the keyboard.

Instantly the ancient fish screen saver that she so loved disappeared and a copy of Steve's e-mail appeared on her screen. She'd been staring at it off and on for the last three hours, afraid to actually log on and see what other mail he had left her.

> FOUND BACK DOOR. NEED CREATIVE EXPERT. SUCCESS EQUALS BIG BUCKS. OTHERWISE PAYS HOURLY FOR ONE WEEK'S WORK, AS MANY HOURS AS YOU CAN CRAM. YOU'RE THE BEST FOR THIS ONE, HON. IT'S YOUR DOOR.
>
> LOVE,
> EVIL K'STEVIL
> MASTER OF DARING-DO

Master of Illegal Do-Do was more like it. She had thought, when she moved to Shasta City, that she had gotten far away from everything. From Travis's harebrained schemes and New Age San Francisco friends, and from the Silicon Valley Nerd Group, who had once been her salvation and who had turned into her greatest nightmare.

And her greatest temptation.

She bit off the crust, then spat it out. Burned, just like the last time. That was the bad thing about small towns. They had terrible pizza. She hadn't thought her choice of location through, either. She had loved driving through Shasta City on her way to vacations in Oregon. The town was small and cozy, with skiing in the winter and boating in the summer. Mount Shasta's icy top was a presence in and of itself and somehow felt like an old friend. Her favorite restaurant in the whole world was in Shasta City, a fine dining place in a house just off the freeway, a place she had often imagined herself sitting in, drinking a double tall, and reading the latest Gibson.

What she hadn't realized when she moved was that in the winter, there were no jobs in Shasta. And only people with real incomes could afford to sit in restaurants or go skiing. She had three jobs lined up for spring, all of them waiting tables—what else could a high school grad get?—but spring was still several months away.

A hundred dollars to her name and nothing left to sell. Her vinyl collection had gone first, for a minuscule amount of money on the face of it. Her collectible glasses went next—all except the Burger King set from the first *Star Wars* movie, a set she had searched all of Southern California for and couldn't bear to part with. In the end, she'd even sold her books, the most wrenchingly painful experience she had ever gone through in her life. Two thousand volumes, all in mint condition, all science fiction. With that money, she had paid her lawyer's retainer, rented the U-Haul, and lived for four months in Shasta City.

The unpacked boxes were filled with the not-so-essentials she'd managed to steal from her life with Travis. Her flatware and stoneware—a set for twelve, in case she ever had a dinner party. Her cooking equipment. Her wedding dress, and the evening gowns Travis had insisted she buy for his hotline "galas." Her technical manuals, and a few things from her childhood, including a copy of *Brigadoon* she'd gotten from the lawyer who got her mother off on that murder charge.

She needed Big Money. She needed small money.

And, if she was honest with herself, she needed the challenge, to get her mind off the lonely mess her life had become.

Besides, this was the only hacking project that had ever interested her. And Steve knew it.

Steve. She'd thought him exciting when he'd joined the Nerds. He was handsome in an intellectual sort of way—the kind of guy whose athletic build hinted at an ease with his body, whose dark brown eyes glinted with intelligence, and whose mismatched clothing showed a disinterest in vanities of the flesh. He'd shown her more about computers than her programming friends had shown her in years, and he'd been the one to give her consulting job after consulting job in various companies all across the valley. Of course, since she'd been a contractor, she'd done the work at home and been paid in cash. It wasn't until she sent out résumés listing her contacts that she realized no one had a record of her work, and no one could vouch for her.

Except Steve. And by that point, he had gone underground. The FBI was after him because he had illegally broken into some sensitive computer systems. Steve, always a guy to land on his feet, managed at that point to turn his illegal activities into a profit. He became the guy who could break into any system—for a price.

She was never certain how many of her "consulting" jobs had simply been covers for some of Steve's activities.

And now he wanted her help. She had told him, before she left Travis, that she wouldn't do anything illegal. But this was tempting.

And, if she were honest with herself, it was more than the money.

It was the job.

One afternoon, six months before she left Travis, she had been doing a project for Steve. She was working in what was then Steve's office, a building that had been condemned years before, after the '89 Oakland earthquake. The building swayed on occasion, and once ceiling tiles had fallen near her, but Steve wasn't worried. He had phone lines hooked into what was then a state-of-the-art hybrid PC, and had set up systems that routed his calls through six different continents and seventeen countries. She had been running numbers for him—dialing unlisted government-issue numbers—noting those that answered with modem or fax tones.

Then, on a number with a 505 area code, she had received both a modem tone and this message on her screen:

DR. FULLER! YOU'RE BACK!

Sammi Jo had noted the number. It was in New Mexico. Then, because the computer actually seemed happy to hear from someone, because she was glad for the distraction, and because Fuller had been her maiden name, after all she typed:

I WAS NEVER GONE.

The cursor blinked silently for several minutes. Sammi Jo was about to break the connection when this message appeared on the screen.:

BUT YOU ARE GONE, SAMMI JO. AND I, FOR ONE, MISS YOU.

She broke the connection then and stared at the screen for a long time. Finally, Steve returned. He was as flabbergasted as she was. He printed up the dialogue, then redialed the number.

It had been disconnected.

He traced the number, through some system he had never explained to her, and discovered it connected to a government research lab in Stallion's Gate, New Mexico. He examined all the information he could find on the project. It was classified. He even sent another friend to the area because he was so intrigued, but no one would talk to her.

During those months, he referred to the project as Sammi Jo's ghostly companion. Once he even said that Travis's psychic friends had put a curse on her so that computers all over the country would recognize the touch of her electronic fingers.

She didn't like the jokes, even though she had smiled through them. When she'd first married Travis, all of his friends had made fun of her talk of ghosts and psychic events, even though they were supposed to believe in them. They'd also made fun of her accent and her high school nickname. When they'd moved to California, she'd asked Travis to stop calling her Dixie, and to start calling her Sammi Jo. She had cleaned up the lazy grammar she had fallen into all those years ago as a subtle way of rebelling against her mom. Those changes had gained her a surprising amount of respect. But they didn't dull the hurt when someone made a ghost joke at her expense.

Besides, the computer made her nervous. She felt as if that computer knew her, and really did miss her. She played with other 505 numbers during her free hours in Steve's office, hoping to get the same result.

Now, these many months later, Steve had finally found the back door. He was certain it led to Sammi Jo's ghost computer. If she was able to hack her way in and leave no trace, he would pay her a lot of money for the information she received.

She took a sip of her Diet Coke.

Money.

The ghost computer.

Real work.

And someone who missed her. She couldn't forget that. Someone out there who seemed to actually care. Even if it was a computer, and even if it had the wrong Sammi Jo.

She hit three buttons on her keyboard and listened to the familiar multitone as she logged on. She punched in the return path for Steve's e-mail (today's address, she thought wryly) and typed:

TO: EVIL K'STEVIL
FROM: GHOST GIRL

CONDITIONAL YES. IF YOU PROVIDE BIG BUCKS FOR ONE WEEK'S WORK AND *BIGGER* BUCKS FOR SUCCESS. CALL ME, WE'LL TALK DOLLARS. AND REMEMBER: IF THIS IS AS RISKY AS MOST OF YOUR PROJECTS, I CHARGE TRIPLE.

LOVE & HUGS,
GG

Then, her mission accomplished, she logged off.

Steve knew how she hated to break the law. He also would never pay her triple the going rate. She grabbed the warm Diet Coke and eased off the chair, regretting that she would have to find another source of money, and relieved that her immediate problem was solved.

CHAPTER EIGHT

Here's to you and yours,
No forgettin' us an' oors;
An' whenever you an' yours
Comes to see us an' oors,
Us an' oors'll be as guid
To you and yours,
As ever you an' yours
Was to us an' oors,
Whenever us an' oors
Cam to see you an' yours.
—SCOTTISH TOAST

Loch Ness, March 14, 1986.

Sam couldn't wait for Al. He would have to act on his own. He paused at the base of the stone stairs and glanced at the trickle of water running down the wall. Above, the voices still spoke softly.

He had had the right idea. He needed to talk to Travis, to come up with some sort of compromise.

And he wanted to see Dixie again.

Sam took a deep breath. The whole hall smelled of mildew. He felt as if he had swallowed dust. He tried to stifle a cough, couldn't, and the sound exploded in the small space.

Above him, the conversation stopped abruptly. They knew he was below. Sam sighed and started up the stairs. This was the hardest part of Leaping—choosing the path. What felt right might be completely wrong. He didn't know Dr. Harding's history with Travis, and some of Dixie's comments bothered him. She seemed too genuine to make baseless accusations.

The upstairs was silent, as if the couple were waiting to see what he'd do. He rounded the steps, nearly tripped on the odd stone corner, and had to duck beneath an ancient overhang. The second floor was an addition. The whitewashed walls looked old, but nowhere near as old as the stone.

The stairs ended in a long, narrow hallway. Most of the doors were closed, but one was open. He headed there.

Travis stood by the narrow double bed, the quilt thrown haphazardly over its unmade sheets. A dresser with a washing pitcher and bowl stood to one side, a chair to the other. A tiny plastic model of Nessie stood in the middle of the bowl, only its head and tail extended from the water. Dixie sat on the ledge of the only window, overlooking the loch.

When she saw him, she crossed her arms and turned her back, the movement so like Abagail it took Sam's breath away.

"Look," he said, feeling awkward and too large for the narrow room. "We got off on the wrong foot. This trip—"

"Was a mistake," Travis said. "Dixie and I are going to go home."

Sam looked between them. Dixie's back was rigid. Travis had his fists clenched. Al hadn't said anything about them leaving. He had said that the trip had gone badly, but not that it had ended abruptly.

"Come on, Dad. You had to know this would happen."

Sam licked his lips. "I, um—"

"He don't care," Dixie said.

The way she said it, partly defiant, partly challenging, moved him. What year was this? Eighty-six? And the girl looked about twenty. His heart was fluttering. Something hovered on the edge of his Swiss-cheesed memory, wrapped in a line from *Brigadoon*—

He shook himself, knowing he'd lose them, knowing he had to get back to this conversation, and figure out the riddle of the girl later.

"No," he said. "You're wrong. I care. I wouldn't be here if I didn't."

"You wanted to see what your wacko son was up to now," Travis said. "You wanted to know how bad it was this time, what you'd have to do to get him out of it, didn't you?"

"No," Sam said, but the word sounded as confused as he felt. Travis crossed the room and put his hand on Dixie's arm.

"You're right," he said. "Let's go."

"No!" This time, Sam put force into the word. "You weren't ready to leave a few moments ago, Travis. This is both a test and a way to avoid real conversation."

Travis froze, his back rigid. Dixie moved her head slightly, so that Sam could see her face. Behind that young exterior was a smart, determined woman. He wondered how he'd ever thought her a girl. She raised her chin just a little in a familiar expression—not Abagail's, but—

He wrenched his gaze from hers. "A real conversation," he repeated. "Whether you like it or not."

"We haven't had a real conversation in years," Travis said.

"That's what I was afraid of," Sam muttered.

"You make it sound like my fault," Travis said. "It's not mine. It's yours. Do you know how much I hate the word 'woo-woo'? Or 'wacko'? Or 'idiots'?"

"You used all three about the Loch Ness Monster museum near Drumnadrochit," Dixie said, giving the Scottish word its correct pronunciation. The mix of accents gave the sentence an air of unreality.

They made a good team. Sam felt defensive even though he hadn't been the one who said whatever was said. He swallowed, not wanting to let that defensiveness develop and this conversation to become another full-fledged fight.

He held up a hand. "Let me explain my position," he said, "and then you can explain yours."

Travis crossed his arms and leaned against the wall. "Go ahead," he said.

"I came with you so that we could settle this," Sam said. "Because—"

"Actually, you didn't come with us," Dixie said. "You met us here."

"Because I told him about your birthday," Travis said. "But you even got that wrong, Dad. You were supposed to arrive tomorrow, not yesterday."

"Sorry," Sam said. Harding really had to work on his people skills. "I did come, though, to work this through."

"You came," Dixie said, " 'coz you always

wanted to see Scotland and you needed a break from research, isn't that what you said? Them two things?''

Donald Harding had not made this easy.

''I'm not going to argue every point,'' Sam said. ''I did come here to settle this, no matter what was said in the past. I know this search is important to you, Travis. I know that. But your idea, and the research grants you'd need, make things difficult for me. In my profession, people who espouse unpopular causes sometimes lose credibility. The very thing you want me to lend to the project might be the thing we lose.''

''You lose,'' Travis said tightly.

''We lose,'' Sam said. ''If I lose credibility, I can't add it to your work.''

Travis remained still, only his eyes moving as he studied Sam's face. Dixie bit her lower lip, watching Travis consider Sam's words. She had an opinion about them, that was clear, and it was even clear which direction her opinion went.

She didn't believe him, and the more Sam learned about Donald Harding, the less he believed as well.

''Why would you want to?'' Travis asked. ''Why would you want to add credibility to my work? You haven't even called it work in the past.''

''Isn't that why you asked me along?'' Sam asked. ''Isn't that why we're here, to see if there's any justification in financing such a large venture?''

''I want your help with money, Dad, that's all.''

''That's not all,'' Sam said. ''To get monetary help takes effort. And that effort would require me to use my reputation.''

''And that's what you're worried about? Your reputation?'' Travis's tone was sarcastic. Sam was losing him.

"In theoretical physics,'' Sam said, "reputation can be everything.''

"So you don't want to put your name on the line for something as screwy as the Loch Ness monster. That's why you insisted on this fishing expedition, because you could manipulate it your way. You could go on the boat, you could take photographs, you could say, 'I was there, but I didn't see anything.' And you could then show me how the other photos were faked, and make me feel stupid, all the time protecting your precious reputation.''

Sam swallowed. That probably had been Donald Harding's plan. But it wasn't his. "I just didn't want this to backfire on us,'' he said.

"It already has.'' Travis pushed off the wall with one foot, then brushed past Sam.

"Travis, wait. We're not done—''

But Travis was already down the stairs. Wonderful avoidance tactics. Having the last word by making it impossible for someone else to say anything at all.

"If you argued like that in the beginning,'' Dixie said, "he mighta listened to you. Now's kinda late, don't you think?''

He turned. She was in the same position, watching him. Arms crossed, chin out. She looked defiant and strong.

"I just get a sense that this might be our last chance,'' Sam said.

"You got that right.'' She slipped off the windowsill. She was smaller than he had initially thought, coming up only to his shoulder, her bones delicate, her movements graceful. "Why do you keep staring at me as if you never seen me before? Because the mouse can speak in full sentences?"

"Wh-What's your real name?" he asked, then knew he'd made a mistake.

She rolled her eyes. "You don't remember nothing, do you?" She picked up a candle from the end table near the bed, slapping the holder against her palm as if she held a truncheon. "Or did you just not bother to learn it? That would be typical. You know nothing about Travis. Why should I expect you to know something about me?"

Sam winced. He supposed he deserved that. Or Donald Harding deserved that. What man failed to learn the name of his son's girlfriend?

She sighed and set the candle down. "Samantha," she said softly. "My name is Samantha."

Hearing her speak her name rattled him. A flash of memory—*I saw her!*—faded as soon as it hit.

"Are you all right?" she asked.

His consternation must have shown on his face. He smiled, even though the look felt small and ineffectual, and nodded.

"You don't look all right," she said. "You've looked different all day. My gramma used to say sometimes strangers could rent our bodies. You look like that done happened to you."

He started. His throat was dry. How had she known? Or was it just a quaint cliché that he had never heard before?

"I feel a little different today," he said, not daring to say more. "I'd like to settle things with Travis before I leave."

"Before *you* leave?" she asked. "You were supposed to stay through the week, Dr. Harding."

"I know," he said, even though he didn't. "What can I do? How can I reach him?"

"Shorta what he wants?" she asked.

Sam nodded.

"Nothing," she said. "Nothing at all."

CHAPTER NINE

It occurs to me that this meddling energy—everyone putting in his ten cents' worth and struggling for dominance—is at the heart of the American Genius. It produces results because it creates such pressure, even fear, that people come up with ideas simply to survive. It's the dialectic gone crazy; a hundred theses and antitheses struggling, like spermatozoa, to make it as the synthesis. It's undoubtedly effective when the agreed purpose of the exercise is something simple like maximizing profits; less useful when you are trying to see the woods for the trees. And quite catastrophic when you are looking for light at the end of the tunnel.

—MICHAEL BLAKEMORE

Stallion's Gate, New Mexico. Now.

Al pushed open the door to the Waiting Room, letting the cool blues and whites overwhelm him. He felt oddly exhausted, like he sometimes did after a long session in the Imaging Chamber. Ziggy had once explained that the exhaustion was an aftereffect from switching time lines. Al felt it because he could sometimes remember the shifts. To everyone else, life continued on as usual.

He had let go of the handlink, but in its place he was carrying a pocket-sized mirror. His fist was closed over the mirror, so no one else could see it.

He wasn't sure if this plan would work, but he had to try. He couldn't rid himself of the fear at the pit of his gut. They'd lost Sam, and they wouldn't be able to get him back without help. The last time Al had gone for help in the Waiting Room, it had been from his own, younger, self. The time before that, he'd had to rig the Imaging Chamber so Katie McBain could testify at her own rape trial. Both of those events had somehow seemed less stressful than this one.

Perhaps because he was breaking all the rules.

Verbena Beeks sat in a wooden chair beside the bed. She had a clipboard in her lap, a pen in hand. When Al saw her, he had a strange duality of thought. She and Dr. Fuller had been working on a new interview technique because Dr. Fuller thought the switching process was critical to understanding Project Quantum Leap. Overlaid above that thought was this one: Dr. Beeks felt frustrated because she did little more than counsel the staff, protect the visitors, and work to keep everyone sane. She wanted, more than anything, to help bring Sam home.

Al shook his head, knowing that the two time lines had just crossed in his mind. The knot in his gut tightened as he closed the door behind himself.

Dr. Beeks turned and smiled at Al. But he wasn't looking at her. He was looking at the man in the bed.

For a reason that Ziggy had yet to explain, Al usually saw the visitors in the Waiting Room as themselves rather than as Sam. He knew the others, like Dr. Beeks, saw Sam's body being used in different ways. Al's private theory was that because of his mental hookup with Sam, he was able to see the reality behind the illusion. That had only backfired once or twice, especially the time Sam had Leapt into that goddess of love, Samantha Stormer. Al didn't want to think about the confusion *that* Leap had caused for him.

The man in the bed was in his fifties, balding, and about fifty pounds overweight. His eyes were too small for his face. He had a prominent chin and five o'clock shadow.

"Are you going to ask me ridiculous questions too?" the man asked.

Al smiled. Belligerence was common, especially once a visitor realized he or she wasn't sick. "I'm Admiral Al Calavicci. And you're Dr. Donald Harding, the physicist, am I right?"

"Admiral . . ." Dr. Beeks said in a cautioning tone.

"That's right." Harding propped himself on one elbow. "What's the military got to do with this?"

"Quite a bit, actually," Al said. "But you'll have to humor me for a moment. I may repeat some of the questions that Dr. Beeks has already asked you."

"I don't think so," Dr. Beeks said. To someone who didn't know her, she sounded calm, but Al heard the underlying note of frustration. "Dr. Harding is more concerned with where he is than with my questions."

"I think I can help with that." Al came up behind Dr. Beeks's chair. "That'll be all, Dr. Beeks. I'll call you if I need you."

As Dr. Beeks stood, she shot him a look filled with warning, worry, and wrath all mixed together. She let herself out of the Waiting Room without so much as a backwards glance.

"She was asking pretty strange questions," Harding said.

"I know." Al slipped into her chair. "We're running an unusual program here."

"What kind of program?" Harding asked.

"In a moment," Al said. "First, tell me the last thing you remember."

Harding sat up. Al got a sense that the man hadn't been this animated for Dr. Beeks. "I was on Loch Ness," Harding said, "in the pouring rain, and the damned Scot was pretending the engine was down."

"Looking for the monster?" Al asked.

To Al's surprise, Harding flushed. "It's my kid's idea. He wants me to sponsor some seminar on the monster."

"Seminar?" Al asked. That information was different from the information he'd gotten from Ziggy—in one or another time line.

"I don't know," Harding said. "It's some woo-woo scam to rip money from the legitimate scientific community. You probably don't understand, Admiral, how difficult it is to get money for real scientific projects. But when they get diluted by wacko schemes of the intellectually challenged, then things become even more difficult."

Al did understand. He understood too well. But he also remembered when those charges had been leveled at the Project itself. He had to literally bite his tongue to stop going down that side road. It might become important when he reestablished contact with Sam, but not until then.

"What's the date, Doctor?" Al asked.

"March 14, 1986." Harding's gaze narrowed. "I know I don't have any injuries, but both you and that shrink asked the same question. What gives?"

"One more question," Al said. "Are you familiar with a woman named Samantha Fuller?"

"Samantha Fuller. No, I—wait, yes, that's the name of the piece my son's been squeezing. Only he calls her Dixie. What's your interest in her, Admiral?"

Al patted his pocket for a cigar, then realized he didn't have one—a pocket or a cigar. He had remembered the mirror, but not the cigar. Big mistake. He bit his lower lip and reminded himself that most scientists were not like Sam. Most were what Al called genius geniuses—folks who spent so much time living in their brains they had no sense of the real world, or of manners, for that matter—not genial geniuses, like Sam.

"Admiral?" Harding's tone had gotten lower. He was sitting on the edge of the bed, looking oddly vulnerable in the white Fermi-Suit.

"Do you know Dr. Samuel Beckett?"

"The playwright or the physicist?"

Al smiled. Maybe there was some hope for Harding yet. Most scientists never caught the literary reference.

"The physicist," Al said. "And actually, he's more like Godot these days than anything else."

"Waiting on him, are you?" Harding asked, and chuckled.

Al didn't laugh. Sam's inability to come home wasn't something Al found funny. "Yes," he said. "We are. And therein lies the problem." He wasn't sure how he was going to explain this. He just knew he had to. "We need your help, Doctor, as well as your ability to maintain confidentiality."

"Most of my grants have come from major research labs, Admiral. I am an expert at silence."

Al took a deep breath. He had only done this a few times before, and each time it had been difficult. "Then listen," he said, "because this might be hard. Dr. Beckett used your theories, as well as several others, in creating a project we called Starbright. He theorized that a man could travel through time during his own lifetime—"

"I read Dr. Beckett's research." Harding sniffed, as if time travel belonged in that wacko, woo-woo category inhabited by the monster.

"Then I don't need to explain the details to you," Al said, relieved. He hadn't been certain he had enough grasp of the science to discuss it with another theoretical physicist. "All I need to do is tell you that Dr. Beckett was right."

"And now he's got some graduate assistant stuck in 1955, and because this is government funded, you're here. You brought me in somehow, and we need a consult."

"You have the consult right," Al said, "as well as the government funding. The problem, though, is a bit more complicated. You see, you've come forward thirteen years into your future, and you're wearing Dr. Beckett's body. You and Dr. Beckett have effectively switched places, at least for the time being."

Harding glanced down at his hands. Then he looked at the rest of his body, ran fingers over his scalp, touched his face. "Seems like me," he said.

Slowly Al opened his hand. He slid the mirror forward, carefully, so that Harding could see the reflection of the room before he saw the reflection in the mirror.

Harding picked up the mirror, and frowned.

Even though he looked like a fifty-year-old man to Al, Al knew that Harding was seeing Sam's angular face, Sam's strong jaw, Sam's full head of hair.

"No," Harding whispered. "It's not possible. Beckett's research was flawed."

"His first published research was flawed," Al said. "But subsequent work was quite convincing, and it remained under wraps. I don't think anyone outside of the Project here in Stallion's Gate ever saw it."

"But something happened," Harding said. His voice was shaking, but he seemed to be doing an admirable job of ignoring the strangeness of the situation.

"Something happened," Al said, and set about explaining the unusual problems of Project Quantum Leap.

CHAPTER TEN

We are all in the gutter, but some of us are looking at the stars.

—OSCAR WILDE

Mount Shasta, California, Now.

The computer meowed.

Sammi Jo blinked awake. Her neck was cramped. She'd fallen asleep in her chair again. The room smelled of cold pizza, and the only light was the bluish white glare from her screen. The boxes looked like tiny mountains in the gray-blue light.

She had e-mail. That's what the alarm told her.

The computer meowed again, and she wished, for the thousandth time, that she'd taken the cat with her. She'd left her with Travis, just like she'd left everything else, but she had forgotten that she'd recorded the cat's indignant meow for her computer's error/alarm message. Now, every time the message sounded, it made her lonely. But it was one of the few links she had with the outside world, a link she wasn't about to break.

Not yet.

Not until she had some others.

She rubbed the sleep from her eyes, stretched, and sat up. Her shirt felt clammy. She would have to break that hundred to do laundry. She wouldn't be able to get a job otherwise.

She took a sip of warm Diet Coke, winced because it was flat, and then scooted her chair toward the computer. She had remained logged on, something she hadn't done since she moved, afraid, she supposed, that Travis would find her.

Or maybe afraid that he wouldn't.

She hit a command so that the e-mail appeared on her screen.

> OKAY, YOU'RE IN, DOLL. I'LL SEND INFO VIA COURIER. REMEMBER THE SECRET HANDSHAKE? THE DECODER RING PASSWORD? IF NOT, THIS IS A NO-GO.
>
> LOVE,
> S. T. EVEN

She blinked and reread the e-mail, then resisted the urge to pinch herself. This wasn't a dream. Steve had gone for the money without a qualm.

She could have asked for more.

She should have asked for more.

That made her even more nervous. If he hadn't balked at this kind of money, what did he see in this project?

She shook her head, then pushed the hair out of her eyes. He would find her because she had a listed number. She remembered the secret code—she'd helped him establish it: A knock, and when the door opened, the courier would ask, ''Hey, are you Mara?'' She would say yes, and the courier would start singing "It's a Small World." If she gasped and asked him to quit, the courier would know it wasn't safe. And if she smiled and said, "How'd you know that's my favorite song?" the courier would hand her the package. Simple, brilliant, she thought, since most people would slam the door on the courier, or at least ask him to stop singing. *No one* over the age of five would ever admit to liking that song.

She knew Steve hadn't used the code in months, but somehow that made it seem even more secure. What bothered her was that he was going to use a courier at all. No phone contact, no e-mail instructions, no encoded messages. Just good, old-fashioned hard copy, passed from one hand to another.

That meant a great deal was involved.

The hair rose on the back of her neck. She was interested, in spite of herself.

She leaned forward and typed e-mail to the new address Steve had used above.

> IF I'D KNOWN YOU'D BE THAT FLEXIBLE ON THE CASH,
> I'D HAVE ASKED FOR MORE. SOUNDS MAJOR.
> LOVE,
>
> DYING POOR & BROKE IN HOBOKEN

She sent the e-mail, searched through her remaining things, and found one last T-shirt. She had gotten it at Coney Island. From far away, the picture looked like a giant hot dog in a bun. Up close, it became clear that the "dog" in the bun was a dachshund. She'd loved the shirt once, but found that when she wore it, too many people stared at her chest and laughed.

After she found the shirt, she got in the shower,

which was the biggest thing about the apartment, and scrubbed until the hot water was gone.

When she emerged and dressed, she wrapped a clean towel around her neck and let her hair drip on it. More e-mail was waiting for her. It had been sent moments after hers.

> ALL RIGHT, QUADRUPLE THE USUAL RATE, BUT THAT'S MY LAST OFFER. PITY ONLY WORKS ONCE. REMEMBER, I NEED RESULTS WITHIN THE WEEK.
>
> LOVE,
> FAGAN

In response, she typed,

> YOUR GENEROSITY ASTOUNDS ME.
>
> LOVE,
> OLIVER

She stared at the message for a moment before she sent it. That was true. His generosity did astound her. He had always been stingy. The financial plight of his programmers was as unimportant to him as the effect of pollen count on fleas. Maybe he was buying her silence. Or maybe he actually cared.

Tears rose in her eyes and she blinked them back. He didn't care. No one cared. She had learned that much from Travis. The marriage hadn't ended in some great passionate fight. He hadn't even found another woman. He'd simply announced, one morning at breakfast, that they really had nothing in common, and his love for her had faded over the years.

It would be better for both of them if they went their separate ways.

And she had been so hurt, so stunned, she had

taken it all as her fault. She hadn't been interested enough in his work, supportive enough. She had insisted on scientific bases for his studies, even when the psychic hot line came along. When she realized he was hiring psychics based on their word only, she had gotten angry, and he had accused her of not understanding.

She had understood. She knew that there were real psychics in the world—her grandmother had been one of them, whether she wanted to admit it or not—and she knew there were frauds. Travis always gravitated toward the frauds.

A knock on the door made her jump. No one had ever knocked on her door before. Not here. She brushed her wet hair back and took a deep breath.

Show time.

She turned on the interior overhead light and went to the scarred door, blinking in the sudden brightness. She attached the chain and pulled the door open as far as the chain would allow.

"Yes?"

"Mara?" The courier was her height. He wore a motorcycle helmet and scuffed leathers. In his left hand, he held a manila envelope. In his right, he had an electrician's bag.

"That's me."

He smiled. "Small world."

She shook her head and started to close the door, when his booted foot blocked it. Then he ripped off the helmet, and she found herself staring at Steve's flushed face. His hair rose in tufts and the tattoo he'd gotten on his cheek in '96 blanched white as he grinned.

"You're not going to make me sing that damned song, are you?" he asked.

"It's my favorite," she said, and undid the chain. She pulled the door open, and launched herself into his arms, never so happy to see anyone in her whole life.

He twirled her and set her on the stoop. A cool breeze ruffled her damp hair, and she was surprised to see that it was midday, and sunny. The mountain was up behind him, looking powerful and cold in the crisp air. She really should raise the blinds more often.

"This is the ass-end of nowhere," he said.

She didn't answer. He had no right to talk. Some of the places he'd lived had been even worse. "I didn't expect you," she said. "I just sent you e-mail."

"It's only a few hours up the freeway, and I wanted to see how you were doing," he said. "Can I come in?"

"It's a mess."

His smile was tender. "You're a programmer. That goes without saying."

She led him inside, closing the door behind them. She hadn't realized how pathetic the interior looked. The old-fashioned living room with its computer-covered table and single chair, the open door to the bedroom revealing the mattress on the floor, the pizza boxes strewn all over the kitchen, the unpacked boxes everywhere. Steve put his electrician's bag on the easy chair—the only open space—and looked at her.

"Hell, babe, if I'd known it was this bad, I'd've given you something sooner. How come you don't come home to Uncle Steve?"

"I've always liked Mount Shasta City," she said.

"Yeah." His tone was sarcastic. "I can tell."

She didn't like his concern. "Isn't it a risk for you to be here?"

"Why?" he asked. "I've come to see a friend."

"Who used to work for you."

He grinned and set the helmet beside the electrician's bag. "There's no proof of that. As far as the world knows, you're Travis Harding's ex-wife, which puts you in the paranormal camp, about as far from a techie as you can get."

"That's not true," she said, bristling. That was Travis's argument and it was wrong. A person could be technically oriented and still believe in the unexplained. Perhaps believe in the unexplained even more, when you consider all that could go wrong with a computer.

"What's true doesn't matter," Steve said. "All that matters is what people believe." He still hadn't let go of the manila envelope. "So, when we're done here, I'll take you out to dinner and we can make nice."

She raised an eyebrow. Steve had never professed interest before.

"In case someone is watching," he said.

"Oh." She smiled. "Then you'd better make this as datelike as possible, and take me to the best restaurant in town."

"Which is what, the McDonald's just off I-5?"

"No," she said. "Lily's." The place she had moved here for. The place where she'd imagined herself whiling away afternoons, sipping coffee and reading a good book.

"Done," he said, "if you promise to wear something other than that Coney Island T-shirt."

She grinned. She did have her all-purpose black dress. Made of polyester, it never wrinkled. She hated it but at least it was clean.

"So hand over the envelope," she said.

He shook his head. "Not till we're set up. I'm going to tamper with your phone line, then I'm going to add one of my boxes to your computer. No one should be able to trace you."

"I know the drill," she said.

"Not this drill." He reached into the electrician's bag and pulled out a box the size of his palm. "On the side here is a switch with six settings. If you think someone's on to you, you switch the settings. You only have seven chances, but I'm gambling that it'll take anyone at least a day to trace through all the systems."

That chill was covering her again. "What are we breaking into?" she asked.

"You don't want to know," he said.

"I do. You've never offered so much money before."

"It's federal."

"The government?" Her voice squeaked. "If I get caught, that's worse than a felony, that's—"

"My problem," he said. "I'll pay your legal bills."

"Right," she said. "Like you'll even be in the country." She swallowed, knowing how much money she was turning down, and how desperately she needed every penny. "I won't do it."

"Come on, Sam. I need you."

"Get one of your other stooges to do this. I told you. I draw the line at illegal."

Steve sighed and set the box down. "My other

stooges have tried it. They get the same prompt you got. Then they get hang-ups and an instant trace. A few have managed to convince the computer they just dialed a wrong number, but most have resulted in a loss of access. I only have a few pages of numbers left, Sam. It's not like you're breaking into the military or anything. It's research."

"Research. Government funded." She crossed her arms. "Like weapons. And I suppose you have some shady international agency putting up the funds."

"No, it's not weapons," he said. "It's time travel. And I have a major think tank that wants the information and can't get it because it belongs to the government."

"So they're relying on illegal means? Nice try, Steve, but even I'm not that stupid."

"They're desperate, Sam, and so am I. I'll pay you six times what I usually do."

She froze. Six times. She'd be able to sit in Lily's for a year on that money, job or no job. "How much are they paying you?"

"Enough to retire," he said.

She let out a breath. "Ten times."

"Sam—"

"Ten times," she repeated. "You're asking me to break the law. You're asking me to compromise my ethics, and if something goes wrong, you're asking me to be the fall guy."

"Sam, the work you've done for me has never been exactly legal."

"Ten times." She crossed her arms. "You can't do it without me."

He sighed and shook his head, defeated. "You're right," he said. "I can't."

CHAPTER ELEVEN

> He is gone on the mountain,
> He is lost to the forest,
> Like a summer-dried fountain,
> When our need was the sorest.
> —SIR WALTER SCOTT

Loch Ness, March 14, 1986.

The rain had stopped. Sam went outside and stood on the inn's porch. The sky was still overcast, and the loch looked gray. Nothing stirred on its surface. He sighed. He almost wished for something large to break through, a glimpse of a head, a tail, a spiny backside, so that he could say to Travis, ''All right. I believe. Let's move on.''

A cool breeze ruffled his hair. The air had that fresh after-rain smell, mingling with the natural scent of the loch. The wild beauty of the place gave him a sense that if he let himself, he could believe in anything here. The land around him had a timelessness that evoked the feel of history, a feel he never got in his own country—not even when he'd spent a few days as his own great-grandfather in the American Civil War.

He leaned forward and put his hands on the wooden rail. Its slippery cool dampness felt good on his palms. He thought over his situation. He had no Al, not since that apparent difficulty with Ziggy. He had no real direction. And he did have Dixie, the girl who looked like Abagail.

The answer to the riddle of Dixie lay inside his Swiss-cheesed memory, he knew, inside his stuttering brain. He would have the answer soon—he was certain.

"Are ye lookin' for the young lad?"

The voice was female and the Scottish accent so thick it took Sam a moment to understand that the woman was talking to him. He turned. The woman behind him was solidly built, and about the same age as Harding. She wore dungarees and a pair of American-made tennis shoes. Her sweater was Scottish, though, with that rich, blended gray wool unique to the Isles. Her face was round and her eyes the faded blue of a rain-washed sky.

"I couldna help but hear the fight. 'Tis sad, ye know, when a boy believes only magic will help him. Makes me wonder how 'twas he got that way in the first place." She tilted her head at Sam as if she were a counselor, leading him to the answer.

"I don't know," Sam said. "I wish I did."

She smiled. "Do ye remember how ye felt as a boy, how yer da was both a mystery 'n' a fright 'n' yet the greatest thing on Earth?"

Sam smiled in return. His father had been all of those and more, and he hadn't comprehended Sam's choice to leave the farm for a school as far away as MIT any more than Harding seemed to understand Travis's interest in the supernatural.

"I remember," Sam said.

" 'Tis that way 'twixt fathers 'n' sons. E'en now. Ye canna remake him inta yerself. And ye'll never be the father he wants, na matter what ye do."

Sam leaned against the railing. "How'd you learn all of this?"

She shrugged. " 'Tis the same 'twixt mothers 'n' daughters. I see me mistakes in ye. Dinna make them or ye'll die alone 'n' forgot."

He knew. That was what he was fighting. But she didn't know that. She didn't know why Sam was here.

"You seem too young to be thinking about death," Sam said.

She tugged on her sweater and sighed. "Aye," she said. "But me daughter is long gone and I dinna know where she is. I probably'll never know. Dinna let that happen."

"I'm trying not to," Sam said.

She smiled, but her smile was sad. "Afore taday I wouldna thought it. But taday ye seem like a new man." She nodded with her head toward the loch. "Yer lad is at Urquhart Castle. He dinna even take the lass with him. 'Tis thinking, he is, about leaving, would be my wager. Doesna seem right, him leaving just yet."

"No," Sam said. "It doesn't." He swallowed. "How do I get to Urquhart Castle?"

"I'll show ye," she said.

The trail she pointed out to him wound through the hills, past a dusty road, and behind several disreputable-looking houses. Before they parted, Sam discovered that the woman owned the inn. Her name was

Mrs. Comyn, and the old man on the boat that morning was her father, Angus MacNab. Her mother was long dead, her daughter long missing, and of her husband, she made not a mention. It took most of Sam's talent to extricate himself from her before he could set off down the path.

And she hadn't let him go without a lunch neatly packed in a basket, which he carried over his left arm. He hadn't bothered to look inside—he would do that when he reached the castle and found Travis.

After what seemed like days, though it had probably been an hour at most, he saw the castle on a hill overlooking the loch. Now a ruin, Urquhart Castle looked ancient. Made of brown stone, it almost seemed part of the landscape. The hills rose behind it higher than what was left of the castle. One tower still stood in dilapidated form; of the rest only one story remained. Sam could almost imagine it in its medieval heyday, the center of activity for this part of Scotland, with the laird of the manor sitting in his Great Room, supervising a feast.

He approached from the tower side of the castle. The waters of the loch glistened, even though there was little light. He wondered if there'd been any sightings of the monster from this place, maybe even as long ago as when the castle was built. But he had no way of getting his answer, not without asking Travis, which wasn't something he really wanted to do.

As he approached, he saw a figure move near the top of the ruined tower. On impulse, Sam waved. A hesitant hand went up, executed a curt response, and then went down again.

Travis.

At least Sam had found him.

But as he got closer, the figure disappeared. The castle appeared deserted, and when Sam arrived at the main gate, he was surprised to see a well-built path crossing what appeared to be a moat, leading to a closed and bolted main door.

Sam followed the walkway. It was made of white stone rounded by the passing of thousands of feet. The sense of antiquity he had felt near the inn was magnified here a hundredfold. If he closed his eyes, he felt as if he could actually touch the past.

Neat trick.

Now if he could only touch the present—his real present, the one that would take him back to the Project, Al, and his home.

He stopped at the door. An iron gate, obviously newer than the castle itself, was down over the oak door. He sighed and leaned against the stone.

Maybe he was mistaken, and it hadn't been Travis he had seen at the tower. Perhaps it had been the person who kept the castle, who cleared out the tourists for the night, who guaranteed that everything was safe before the moon rose.

Then he heard the crunching of rock on the walkway and thought the castle's keeper was approaching. He ran a hand over his face, then pushed off the cool stone to his feet, planning to ask about Travis.

But the person he saw appeared on the bridge, as if he'd been outside the castle rather than in the tower—and it was Travis. His thinning hair was windblown, and his cheeks were red with cold.

"Dad? What are you doing here?"

"I wanted to talk to you," Sam said. "I wanted to apologize."

"For what?" Travis asked. "You're no different than you've always been."

"I think I am a little different," Sam said. He held out his hands. "I know you're thinking of leaving, but give me one more chance."

"To what? To make fun of my dream?"

Sam shook his head. "To see it."

Travis's eyes narrowed. He licked his lips, then looked away. "Why? Why would you do that now?"

"Because it's time, Travis." Sam spoke softly. "This might be our last chance."

Travis nodded once, as if he understood. Then he walked toward the main path, stood with his hands on the stone railing, and gazed down. He looked incongruous—his windbreaker was flapping in the breeze while his hands were resting on stones that had been there longer than his own country had existed.

Sam followed, hands in the pockets of his own coat. It was cold here, but not foreboding. The place just seemed to have a perpetual chill.

"I don't know what it'll prove," Travis said softly.

"Maybe it'll prove that we can listen to each other," Sam said.

"Can we?" Travis asked.

Sam shrugged. "I don't know. But I'm willing to try."

Travis turned. He studied Sam's face as if he'd never seen it before. "I am too," he said.

Sam put his hand on Travis's shoulder, and together they walked back to the path that led toward the inn. They had a truce, at least.

It was a start.

But Sam didn't know if it was the right start. He wished Al would return.

He hadn't felt this alone in a long, long time.

CHAPTER TWELVE

The universe looks more like a great thought than a great machine.

—JAMES JEANS

Stallion's Gate, New Mexico, Now.

Harding took the news rather well, considering. He hadn't screamed, hadn't lost his mind, hadn't panicked at all. Instead he had asked a thousand impossible questions and tried to hide the fact that his hands were shaking.

He sat on the edge of the bed, trying to look dignified, trying to pretend that his life hadn't just been altered, that all his preconceptions hadn't been shattered. And he had done a pretty good job, for a man who didn't have a subtle bone in his body.

But Al noticed anyway. He also noticed the rise in the level of tension in the Waiting Room and the deepening flush in Harding's neck. The whole idea was dangerously close to woo-woo, Al thought, not willing to make that comment to Harding, but wanting to.

On some gut level, Al didn't like the man, but he

didn't want to admit it. And whether or not he liked Harding didn't matter. What mattered was the size of Harding's noggin. And compared with everyone but Sam, Harding had impressive smarts.

This was the first time Al had had such an opportunity.

He planned to use it. Not simply to find Sam in this Leap, but to bring Sam home.

No matter about the rules. No matter that dozens of other scientists had been unable to make the theoretical connections that Sam had made. Harding, Sam had once said, was the only theoretical physicist who could understand what Sam had done. Even Sam's old mentor, LoNigro, hadn't been able to keep up with his prize pupil.

And Al needed Harding. More so now that Ziggy couldn't locate Sam.

Al looked at the nervous, overwhelmed man across from him. The temperature in the Waiting Room seemed to have gone up ten degrees from the stress. For once, the blue walls weren't calming anyone, not even Al. He felt ambivalent about what he had just done, even though he felt it justified.

Dr. Beeks would have a field day when she got her hands on Harding. Preferably *after* Al was done with him.

"Well," Al asked, having reached the limits of his ability to explain. "You ready to meet Ziggy?"

"The hybrid computer?" Harding's voice broke, but he didn't seem to notice. Al didn't know if Harding's reactions were coming from fear or fascination or both.

Probably mixed with a healthy amount of disbelief.

Al nodded and stood. He held out a hand to Harding, knowing that the first movement up would be the toughest.

But Harding didn't take the offered hand. He braced himself, then stood slowly. He looked at his body as he stood, then looked away, nearly losing his balance. Amazing how many movements were ingrained into a man based on his size and weight. Harding had gone from a squat, balding, overweight man to a tall, trim one in what seemed to him a heartbeat.

He coped well.

"Let the body do the work," Al said.

Harding nodded once, then walked toward the door. Al stepped ahead of him and opened it. Then he led Harding into the main room.

He had never really looked at the room through a visitor's eyes. Ziggy dominated everything. The room was spare otherwise, and oddly colored, thanks to Ziggy's lighting schemes.

Dr. Beeks was standing in Al's usual spot near Ziggy. Multicolored geometric lights were flashing on the hybrid computer's surface. Gooshie stood behind Dr. Beeks, his face a sickly green as the colors painted his skin. Tina leaned against the door in the back, her red travel suit crumpled. She looked exhausted.

She looked good.

She also looked mad.

At him, probably, for bringing her back early.

"Everyone," Al said, "this is—"

But he couldn't finish. To them, Harding looked like Sam, and as a group their jaws dropped, their eyes opened wider. Dr. Beeks knew, but the others hadn't put it together yet. Tina's eyes filled with tears.

"Dr. Beckett," Gooshie murmured.

''Ah—no,'' Al said. ''Actually, this is Dr. Donald Harding. He's going to help us, if he can.''

Al turned slightly as he spoke. Harding was behind him, one hand on the wall, eyes wider than those of the Project staff. He was staring at Ziggy, at the equipment, at everything with the look of a child who had just seen the largest candy store on the planet.

''This is the hybrid computer?'' he asked softly.

''Ziggy,'' she said. ''My name is Ziggy. It's a pleasure to meet you, Dr. Harding. Dr. Beckett spoke highly of your work.''

''His is quite impressive as well,'' Harding said. He walked into the main part of the room. He didn't seem to notice the chill on his bare feet. Al stepped back and watched. He had never brought anyone to this part of the Project before—at least, not anyone who had the remotest chance of understanding it.

Harding surveyed his surroundings, hands splayed, mouth wide. It would take him a moment to get his bearings.

''Have you found Sam yet?'' Al asked.

Gooshie shook his head. ''We are trying, Admiral. But the time stream is still in flux.''

''Dr. Harding says he came from the same point. Loch Ness, Scotland, March 14, 1986.''

''I have scanned that period and location, Admiral,'' Ziggy said. ''I cannot locate Dr. Beckett's brain patterns.''

''But he's got to be there,'' Al said.

''I'm sorry, Admiral, but he does not have to be anywhere.'' Ziggy's words echoed in the large chamber. She spoke Al's greatest fear—that Sam's consciousness would float away, become untraceable, and they would lose him.

"He's there," Al said.

"If he is, Admiral, the time storm is too powerful for us to be able to read him through it."

"What if I go into the Imaging Chamber?"

"That might make things easier," Ziggy said, then paused delicately. "For me, that is."

"But not for me," Al said. He closed his eyes. He knew what would happen. He had gone through it once before. The time stream had swirled around him so fast he had nearly blown chunks.

"What about me?" Harding asked.

"Yeah," Al said. "We need to get Dr. Harding up to speed as quickly as we can."

"I'm not sure that's a good idea, Admiral," Dr. Beeks said. "We don't know the psychological effects of this sort of dislocation."

Al was willing to say the hell with psychological effects. He was gambling on the fact that they could return everything to normal and Dr. Harding wouldn't remember any of what had happened. But because failure was not an impossibility, he would have to take Dr. Beeks's suggestions under consideration.

"Well?" he asked Harding. "It's your call."

Harding squinted at Dr. Beeks. "You're a psychologist?"

"A psychiatrist, actually," she said.

"I've always thought psychology a pseudoscience. I don't think your questions or concerns are relevant. I would prefer to get to work." Harding's tone was clipped and abrupt. Dr. Beeks was too much of a professional to show any distress, but Al knew how pissed off she was. She'd heard that sort of insult before.

"Dr. Beeks is right," Ziggy said. "You're of no

use to us, Dr. Harding, if you suddenly have a breakdown.''

''I won't break down,'' Harding said. ''I haven't so far.''

''Good point,'' Al said. ''It takes a lot to make some men snap.''

As he should know. He'd watched the Viet Cong break more men than he wanted to think about.

''Tina,'' Al said, ''can you answer some of Dr. Harding's preliminary questions—?''

''I can do that,'' Ziggy said, her tone indicating a slight offense.

''You'll be working with me,'' Al said.

''Yes, Admiral. And I'll be doing several thousand other tasks as well. Unlike humans, I am omnidirectional. I can, in your parlance, walk and chew gum at the same time.''

Al grinned. At last he had her. ''Actually, doll, I believe those are two things you can't do.'' He turned to Harding. ''If I go, you're on your own here.''

''Fine. Go.'' Harding waved a hand.

Al felt a momentary shock. He hadn't expected Harding to dismiss him so easily. But Harding was already leaning over Ziggy's console, staring at the equipment.

Al sighed. Harding and Ziggy. Two supersized egos, working together. It could get ugly.

Or it just might work.

CHAPTER THIRTEEN

Alice laughed. "There's no use trying," she said: "one can't believe impossible things."

"I daresay you haven't had much practice," said the Queen. "When I was your age, I always did it for half-an-hour a day. Why, sometimes, I've believed as many as six impossible things before breakfast."

—LEWIS CARROLL, *THROUGH THE LOOKING GLASS*

Mount Shasta, California, Now.

Dinner helped, and so did the cash. Fifty thousand dollars in hundreds, stacked in bundles. Steve had cautioned her to deposit only a small part of it in her account at one time if she was going to make any deposits at all.

Sammi Jo stood in the center of her cluttered apartment. She had taken off her shoes. The floor was gritty beneath her bare feet. She still clutched her book bag, filled with bundles, and she still wore her black dress.

Steve had been gone for fifteen minutes, and she hadn't moved since he left. She'd been thinking, and obsessing, and trying to figure out a safe place to hide the money. She had never seen so much money in her life. Steve had actually made her count the bundles so that she knew he hadn't cheated her.

He'd never been worried about that before either.

It made her wonder how he had been paid.

That thought terrified her. She had visions of cash bundles in those steel briefcases from all the bad action films she had ever seen.

Steve had told her how to manage the money, but not where to keep it. The best thing she could come up with was a safe-deposit box in her regular bank. In the same bad action films, she had seen people keep cash in those. She might as well, too.

The money, more than anything, convinced Sammi Jo that Steve had hired her to do something illegal. But she rationalized—and she knew it was a rationalization—that she wasn't doing anything more than dialing phone numbers. If she succeeded in breaking into the system he wanted, then she would decide whether or not she'd let him know.

After all, she'd get to keep the money either way.

Besides, she had always wanted to find out who had welcomed her so warmly. And why. If she found that computer again, then she would have to make some decisions. She would have to choose whether or not to give the information to Steve.

By then, she would have traced the company that hired Steve. She would make her own determination.

She set the book bag under a big stack of dirty clothes. If anyone broke into her place, they would take the computer and the equipment, but even if they tossed the clothes, they wouldn't think to look in the book bag. In the morning, she would go to the bank and rent a safe-deposit box.

Tonight, though, she would get to work. She was too intrigued not to.

She pulled out the manila folder, undid the clasp, and removed the sheets of hard copy. Telephone numbers, in several columns of six-point type, faced her. All with the same area code.

For a back door, it looked pretty complicated. She should have asked Steve what made him so sure one of these numbers would lead to her ghost computer.

She turned on the desk lamp beside her computer, tapped the space bar to get rid of the screen saver, and put the first sheet in her scanner. After a few moments, the program beeped. She double-checked the scan. It was clean. She then fed the rest of the sheets through the scanner, made a backup of the new files, and replaced the sheets in the manila envelope. That she placed under the cushion in her only comfortable chair.

Then she hit the dial service on her computer and set her system to dial each number in turn. The modem issued its multitone, the computer beeped as it dialed a number, and she heard a busy signal. It would redial until it got a ring. When someone answered, the computer would notify her that it had received a voice communication. If it got a tone, it would notify her of that. She would have to determine if her computer was talking to a fax, another computer, or both.

She eyed the mattress in the nearby bedroom, wondering if it would be worth lying down. Finally her full stomach convinced her a nap would be appropriate.

It might be the only sleep she'd get all week.

CHAPTER FOURTEEN

A child born at midnight is, also, regarded as being one who will live to be "different"—either for good or for ill. Usually, the child born at midnight, or in the "wee sma' oors," is expected to manifest in later life some peculiar brilliance of intellect, even though such brilliance should be allied to a little wildness.

—RONALD MACDONALD DOUGLAS,
SCOTTISH LORE AND FOLKLORE

Loch Ness, March 14, 1986.

By the time Sam and Travis arrived at the inn, it had grown dark. The air smelled of an earthy dampness. The breeze was still steady and splashed waves against the rocks that lined the loch. Travis turned every time he heard a splash, as if he expected the monster to crawl out of the loch and appear behind them.

They slipped in the main door. The lights were lit in the public room and the large table in the center had three place settings. The rich scents of roasted meat and cooked onions reached them, making Sam's mouth water. Travis wrinkled his nose.

Mrs. Comyn doesn't have to prepare a traditional dish every night,'' he murmured.

''Be thankful it's not haggis,'' Sam said.

Travis peered at him from under a lock of hair. ''You have a pitifully short memory, don't you?''

Sam shrugged, secretly pleased that meal had been inflicted on Donald Harding and not on him.

Mrs. Comyn came through the main door, a pitcher of ale in one hand, tin cups in the other. ''There ye are,'' she said. ''I'd been tellin' the lassie 'twas only a matter a time now. I'll get her. She was helping.''

''Doing what?'' Travis sounded surprised.

''Adding the peas.'' Dixie came out of the back room carrying several pot holders and a serving ladle. ''If you put them in too early, they get mushy. 'N' ye dinna wan mushie peas in yer hotchpotch.''

She did a fair imitation of Mrs. Comyn, who smiled. ''The lass learns fast.'' She nodded her head, then disappeared through the door, saying, ''I'll be bringin' the dinner now.''

''Hotchpotch?'' Travis whispered. ''What sort of torture is that? It's not more sheep, is it?''

''Mutton,'' Sam corrected.

''I thought mutton was sheep,'' Travis said.

''You don't eat sheep,'' Dixie said as she put the pot holders and the ladle in the middle of the table. ''Just like you don't eat cow. You eat beef and you eat mutton.''

''Thank you, Julia Child,'' Travis said.

''I may not be as educated as you, Travis, but I do know some things about the real world.'' She straightened the pot holders so that they would act as a trivet for the pot. '' 'Sides, you're the one who wanted to experience Scotland. And whether you like it or not, they've eaten this stuff for hundreds a years."

"It tastes that way," Travis said. He took a seat at the round table, picked up the pitcher of ale, and poured some into a tin cup.

"So what's hotchpotch?" Sam asked, not certain that he was any more thrilled about Scottish eating habits than Travis.

"Meat, vegetable, and barley stew," Dixie said. "She's been working on it all day, so you should at least pretend to enjoy it."

"What kind of meat?" Travis asked.

"Mutton, lad." Mrs. Comyn came in, carrying a huge serving bowl. The rich smell of cooked food made Sam's stomach rumble. "It's good for ye."

"I'm sure," Travis said, taking a sip of ale.

She set the bowl on the pot holders, put the ladle in, and winked at Sam. "Looks like the walk did ye good," she said.

"Some," he said.

She smiled, ladled food into a bowl, and set it before him. Grease swam on the top, but the broth was a deep brown and the vegetables looked fresh. She served the other two, then disappeared out the door.

Dixie took a bite from her bowl without hesitation. Travis pushed his food around. Sam found some barley and broth and tasted. Salty but surprisingly good. He ate with more gusto than he had originally expected.

"I'm sorry about your birthday," Travis said to Dixie. He sounded contrite. "When we leave here, we'll do it up right."

Dixie flushed. She kept her head down, her concentration on the soup. "It's okay."

"That's right. It's your birthday," Sam said, wondering why no one had made a fuss. His family always had.

Sam closed his eyes and shook his head. He remembered that Donald Harding had interfered with the young couple's plans by arriving early.

"It's okay, really," Dixie said. She sounded almost convincing. Not quite. Like a child who was used to being disappointed, and used to comforting the adults who disappointed her.

"We could do something special," Sam said. "Maybe help Mrs. Comyn make a cake."

Travis looked at him in complete shock. Dixie's flush grew deeper. "Please," she said. "Don't make no fuss over me. Please."

This time she sounded sincere. Forgetting was one thing. Trying to make up for it, apparently, was worse.

No one spoke after that. Sam felt awkward, as if ruining her birthday was his fault, not Harding's. No wonder the man had difficulty with his son. Barging in on a special occasion was inconsiderate, and then berating the trip made the action seem even more mean.

"So," Sam said, deciding that he'd better make conversation. "Travis never really told me how you met."

Dixie looked at Travis over her stew bowl. He shrugged. Sam's guess had been right. Travis *hadn't* told his father how he'd met Dixie.

"If it's not really something you want to talk about," Sam said, "that's—"

"No." Dixie's smile was tight. "You asked."

A chill ran down his spine. Apparently simple questions weren't that simple in this family. Or perhaps the answers skirted things not normally discussed.

"We met in New Orleans," Travis said with a finality that brooked no more conversation.

"That's what you said before," Sam said, making a guess. "I was wondering how."

"You don't want to know, Dad." Travis's voice was soft.

Dixie raised her chin—that familiar gesture again—and said loudly, over Travis's objection, "We met in one of them famous cemeteries, near a special grave."

"The voodoo priestess?" Sam asked, remembering the location of the tomb, remembering the location of the cemetery, but unable, in his Swiss-cheesed state, to remember the exact name of the priestess.

Both Travis and Dixie stared at him as if he had been a voodoo priestess himself. "How'd you know, Dad?" Travis asked.

"You'd be surprised at the things I know," Sam said. "I haven't led a sheltered life." He took another spoonful of stew and resisted the urge to smile. "You met there, and then what?"

"She took me to the Cafe du Monde. I'd never been. She said everyone who came to New Orleans had to do three things, see the cemeteries, walk the Quarter, and go to the Cafe du Monde."

"Beignets and hot chocolate," Sam said, the memory as vivid as a taste on his tongue.

"Then we talked. And I knew that we were right for each other," Travis said.

Dixie's smile was small and secret. "He was interested in my past."

"Dix . . ." Travis said. There was warning in his tone.

"Your past?" Sam asked.

She nodded. Apparently Dixie had decided to ignore Travis as well. "I saw a suicide when I was a little girl. It was an ugly, vicious crime."

I saw her!

Sam set down his spoon. He'd heard a little girl's voice in his head as clearly as he heard Dixie's now. He swallowed. "That fascinated you?" he asked Travis.

Travis shook his head. "Her grandmother fascinated me."

"The one who said other people could inhabit someone's body?" Sam asked.

Dixie smiled. "She called them walk-ins. She said she had seen one."

"A walk-in."

She nodded. "She said he was my mother's one true love, and he was always there when my mother was in trouble."

Travis shoved his bowl away. "Dixie's family has a history of being 'touched.' "

" 'Touched.' " Dixie laughed, but the sound was bitter. "My gramma was in an asylum, Dr. Harding. That's how touched she was."

The hair was rising on the back of Sam's neck. "But you don't believe she was touched."

"Oh, she was," Dixie said. "Just not in the way that everyone believed. She saw people what wasn't there, called my momma's one true love Sam even though Momma didn't know any Sam, and said he come back to defend my momma in a murder trial." Dixie smiled. The smile was sad. "The man who defended Momma was an old family friend. His name was Larry Stanton, not Sam. My gramma was an interesting woman with a fascinating point of view, but she was touched. And she was harmless.''

Sam felt cold. It all came back to him now—all three leaps: the first, when he had been Clayton Fuller, and he'd saved Fuller's little girl Abagail from dying in a fire; the second, when he'd been Will Kinman and had fallen so deeply in love with the adult Abagail that his heart still hurt; and the last, when he had defended Abagail in the murder of Leta Aider, a murder Abagail's daughter had seen, a murder that was really a suicide.

Abagail's daughter. Who had looked just like Abagail. Who had a photographic memory and an IQ of 194. Who liked *Brigadoon*, just like her daddy, and who had been conceived when Sam was Will Kinman.

She had worked hard at hiding the IQ with the grammar and the nickname, but she couldn't quite cover it up. Not all the time. Nor could she hide the loneliness, the same loneliness that had once haunted Abagail. The loneliness that came from being in the Fuller family. The loneliness that came from being different.

''You're Sammi Jo,'' he whispered.

She squinted at him, eyes narrowed, a small furrow in her brow. Like Abagail's.

His daughter.

She was his daughter.

''Samantha Josephine,'' she said. ''They call me Sammi Jo at home.''

''But she prefers Dixie. What's going on, Dad?'' Travis asked.

Sam's hands, resting on the table, were shaking. He reached out to touch her, then stopped in mid-gesture. To her, he was a potential father-in-law, not her father.

He swallowed back all the sentences:

You've gotten so tall.

You look just like your mother.

You're so beautiful.

Instead he said, wishfully, with hope in his voice, "I thought they said all the women in your family were touched." Because if they were, she might be able to see him. She might be able to see Al. She might understand.

A shutter went down over her eyes, and he could feel her retreat. "Cursed is more like it," she said.

"Dad," Travis said.

Sammi Jo held up her hand. It was long and slender, like his. A musician's hand. He wondered if she played the piano. He wondered why she wasn't in college. He wondered what she was doing here, with a world-famous physicist and his strange son.

"It's okay," she said to Travis. "He don't know how painful that word is in my family. He didn't mean to insult me."

"No," Sam said. "I—I didn't."

But he didn't know how to recover. He could no longer think like Donald Harding. He couldn't even pretend. His heart had moved into his throat, and if he wasn't careful, his eyes would fill with tears.

His daughter. He'd only had a few days with her before. He didn't know how long he'd have with her now.

"Some people still believe in that stuff, Dad," Travis said. His tone was arch, meaning, *I'm one of those people.* And Sam finally understood the attraction. Travis was interested in Sammi Jo not for herself, her beautiful sweet face and strong personality, but for her past, for the mysteries that surrounded her and her family. And she had been attracted back because he accepted the strangeness.

He was interested in my past.

No wonder she had seemed pleased when she said that.

Sam swallowed. "I know," he said. "I know people still believe. There's a lot of things in this world that can't be easily explained." He slid his hands under the table, so their shaking wouldn't be visible. "How come you don't believe your grandmother? About this Sam, I mean."

"Come on," Sammi Jo said. "It's so obvious. She never liked my daddy. So she made up somebody else for my momma. It's not pretty, but it makes sense."

"But wh-what if your grandmother was right?" Sam asked.

Sammi Jo's gaze met his. Again she squinted, as if she were trying to see through him. Finally she picked up her napkin—her hands were shaking too—and dabbed at her mouth. Then she put her napkin over her unfinished bowl of stew.

"I'd say," she spoke quietly, evenly, without meeting Sam's gaze, "that you have more in common with Travis than you think."

Then she stood and left the table.

Travis slid his chair back, tossed his napkin down, and stood. "I thought you were going to try," he said. "And instead you make fun of us."

"I wasn't making fun," Sam said. But by the time he finished the sentence, he was speaking to an empty room. Travis had gone after Sammi Jo, after Sam's daughter.

He groaned and put his head in his hands. No wonder Al had left so quickly. No wonder he hadn't come back. Every time Sam had Leaped into something that directly affected their lives, he'd had problems in his link with the Project. And this one had to be very serious, judging by Al's expression.

The problem was that Sam had already changed things.

He knew that because Al hadn't come back.

Al probably couldn't come back.

Sam had changed something important.

And now he had to change it back.

Because if he didn't, he'd stay.

Here.

With his daughter.

Which might not be so bad.

CHAPTER FIFTEEN

> Well, we think that time "passes," flows past us, but what if it is we who move forward, from past to future, always discovering the new? It would be a little like reading a book, you see. The book is all there, all at once, between its covers. But if you want to read the story and understand it, you must begin with the first page, and go forward, always in order.
>
> —URSULA K. LE GUIN, *THE DISPOSSESSED*

Stallion's Gate, New Mexico, Now.

Events whirled around him, strange events, quicker than the eye could see, yet he had the feeling he'd experienced all of them. Rain on the loch, something rising from the mist, a conversation in a deep brogue about oil discovered in the North Sea. Poverty that looked harder than any he'd ever seen, tourists talking about the monster, and complaints about not sharing the wealth of the Thatcher years. Men shouting "Home Rule!" and shaking their heads over newspapers about its defeat. And through it all, the loch, the loch, the loch, deep and gray and terrifyingly cold.

The modern history of Scotland, coming at him too fast to absorb.

Al was getting dizzy, incredibly dizzy, and still the images swirled around him. Sheep, being birthed, being sheared, being slaughtered. Fishermen arguing with oilmen. The North Sea in the rain, the oil rigs rising from it like prehistoric beasts.

And nowhere did he see Sam.

He couldn't even feel Sam.

Finally, the dizziness became a live thing. It traveled from Al's temples to his feet, pausing long enough in his stomach to make him queasy.

"Ziggy!"

Caps and gowns, caps and gowns, students graduating. Formal ceremonies like he had never seen, celebrating universities founded in the fifteenth century. Important speakers stood before university crests: St. Andrews; Glasgow; Aberdeen; and Edinburgh. All those eager faces—

"Ziggy, I'm going to spew!"

Locals worrying the tourist trade, talking in English so thick it sounded like Gaelic. Americans were rude. Germans deserved no courtesy. The French stank. Japanese had money but no understanding of the culture. And the English—

"Ziggy. Stop the world. I want to get off."

Al groaned. He put one hand on his head, another on his stomach, and tried to shut out the tide of images and feelings. Driving on the wrong side of the road. Pulling over as another car flashed its lights.

"Ziggy! If you don't get me out of here I'm going to ralph!"

"Ralph who?" Ziggy asked, her voice charmingly naive.

"Ralph, puke, vomit! Stop this or I'll spray my lunch all over your tidy room."

The images ended. Al staggered backwards, then sat abruptly.

"If you're going to 'ralph,' " Ziggy said, "I prefer that you do so in the men's room."

"I prefer that I don't do it at all." The room had stopped spinning, but Al hadn't. Gooshie let himself in, crackers clutched in his pudgy hands.

"Admiral," he began as he crouched.

Al held up a warning hand. All he needed was one whiff of Gooshie's breath, and all the self-control would be for nothing. "Don't say anything," he said. "Give me the crackers. I'll be fine."

Gooshie nodded and placed the crackers in Al's hand. Saltines. He hated Saltines. But he crunched a few and swallowed them, letting the bread and salt taste coat his mouth and make his stomach react to something else.

He bowed his head and rested it on his knees. They knew where Sam was. They even knew the date. But no matter how hard they searched, they couldn't find him.

The queasiness was easing, but something had replaced it.

Fear.

If they lost Sam, Al wasn't sure what he'd do. If he separated out the friendship angle, the fact that his best friend would be gone forever, if he separated that out, he had yet another problem.

The budget for Project Quantum Leap was on a six-month review. If the Congressional Oversight Committee got wind of the fact that Dr. Beckett was permanently missing, they would shut the Project down in a heartbeat. And then there would be no chance of getting Sam back. Ziggy would be dismantled, or used for some . . . maybe for some military experiments. Tina would be sent to another project, probably in D.C., and Gooshie—well, Gooshie would go with Ziggy.

And Al would be left alone. With his thoughts, and his failures, knowing he had damned his best friend to an exile that was, in its way, as strange and cruel and inexplicable as the one Al had suffered during the war. The only difference was that Sam wasn't being physically tortured.

Al hoped.

Because not finding Sam's brain pattern, not finding his consciousness anywhere, made Al wonder what had gone wrong this time.

And the loss of Dr. Whatshername led him to think that something else had happened as well.

"Admiral?" Ziggy again. She managed that same tone of concern and contempt that his second wife had achieved in the last days of their marriage. "Should we begin again?"

"No!" Al was on his feet in an instant. His stomach decided that was waaaay too fast and made a small, mutinous attempt to toss the crackers back at Gooshie. "Give my gut a chance to settle."

"As you wish, Admiral, but let me remind you that each moment you waste is a moment in which the time storm grows stronger—"

"Then you come in here. You don't have a stomach."

"Admiral," she chided.

He took a deep breath, put his hand out, and left the Imaging Chamber. And stopped.

Gooshie stood by the door, a box of Saltines in his hand. Dr. Beeks was holding a cup of hot tea that looked like slightly stained water. She held it out to him. Al took it absently, knowing it was supposed to settle upset stomachs. They had given it to him in the orphanage, years ago.

But he wasn't looking at them. He was staring at Dr. Harding. Harding had pulled a chair up to Ziggy's side, and was leaning forward like Sam used to, bent in half, as if he were having an in-depth discussion with the machine.

"Are you all right?" Gooshie asked.

"Give me a few minutes," Al said. He reached into the box and removed some more Saltines. "What gives over there?"

"It is rather unnerving, isn't it?" Gooshie asked. "I never expected to see that again."

"Well, it's not Sam," Al said.

"We know," Dr. Beeks said. "But it looks so much like him—"

"It's not Sam," Al said with greater force this time. He drank all the tea in one large gulp, nearly choked, and made himself continue. He took one step forward, clutched Gooshie's arm, and dragged the poor man with him. That way the world didn't spin.

". . . must assume time is nonlinear," Harding was saying. "Your evidence shows that time lines do exist, and that a man can travel backwards on them in no particular order. But what interests me is this creation of alternate realties which only you can remember."

"What are you suggesting, Dr. Harding?" Ziggy asked. "That I am in some way controlling this experiment?"

"You are the control," Harding said. "And the only constant. You say Jacqueline Kennedy died in a previous time line and Dr. Beckett's actions saved her, but we have no memory of this. We have only your word that time has changed. We have no proof."

"You have me," Al said. He had inched closer to the conversation. The hair was standing on the back of his neck, and he figured this reaction wasn't being caused by his nausea. It was because Harding was close, close to something that was affecting this entire Leap. No one had questioned Ziggy's omnipotence before.

Except Sam.

"Admiral." Dr. Harding leaned back a little. His eyes were bright. "I hadn't realized you were out. What a fun-house ride you had. I got dizzy watching from here."

"You shoulda tried it from the inside," Al said.

"Admiral Calavicci remembers many of the altered events," Ziggy said.

Al let go of Gooshie's arm and made a soft request for a chair. Then he clutched the side of Ziggy's monitor, wishing the room would stop spinning, even a little.

"Yeah," he said, "I remember a lot of them. I remember Jackie Kennedy's death, Doctor. She crawled onto the back of that car, and that snake picked her off like she was skeet. There was no dignified funeral, no rallying point for the country. Instead of that little boy saluting, we had two weeping children raised by Bobby and Ethel Kennedy, and a country that spiraled into a kind of despair that the illusion of Camelot saved us from. No Bobby Kennedy candidacy, just Richard Nixon, unadulterated. No—"

"No Sirhan-Sirhan and Chappaquidick," Harding said.

"Oh, we had Chappaquidick," Al said. "My point is, though, that I remember these alternates. Not all of them. But a lot."

"Hmmm." Harding leaned back in his chair. It groaned. Al wasn't certain if he had imagined that or not.

"Do you believe this discussion relevant to Dr. Beckett's plight, Dr. Harding?" Ziggy asked. Only Al heard the subtext behind the question. Ziggy could sound impatient if she wanted to. And she wanted to know if Dr. Harding was going to be valuable to their current dilemma or if he was merely catching up on the research.

"It might be," Harding said. He leaned forward again, but his hand never left his chin. "You seem to be ignoring these alternate time lines. Some theoretical physicists have postulated that time travel is possible, but that every time we change an event, we create a new universe. For example," he turned to Al as he said this, as if Al were his student, "when Dr. Beckett saved Jackie Kennedy, he created a new universe, one in which she did not die. That's the one we're living in now. But the one in which she did die is continuing as if she hadn't died at all. And in that universe, Dr. Beckett develops Project Quantum Leap, and is running it—"

"No," Ziggy said, her voice soft. "In that universe, Dr. Beckett is trapped in his own project, leaping from life to life within his own lifetime—"

"Because that's the universe we started in," Al said. His dizziness remained, but he ignored it.

"But that supposes that in the other alternate universes, there are other Dr. Becketts, working on Project Quantum Leap,'' Harding said. ''In some of those universes, he would be Leaping, as you call it. In others, he would be stuck in Project Starbright. And in others, he would not have gotten the Project off the ground at all.''

''If that were true,'' Ziggy said, ''I would be able to find him. I have been searching for his brain patterns. I haven't found them.''

''If indeed they are the same in each alternate universe,'' Harding said. He frowned and continued to stroke his chin.

Gooshie set the Saltines box down. It rattled as he did so. Dr. Beeks poured more tea into Al's cup. He smiled at her absently, not sure he liked how this discussion was going. ''I don't see how this can help us,'' he said.

''It brings up some interesting possibilities,'' Gooshie said. ''We could, perhaps, find another Dr. Beckett and bring him here to help us.''

''And how do you propose we do that?'' Al snapped. ''We can't even bring our Sam home.''

Gooshie flushed.

''You don't even know he's missing,'' Harding said.

''We know he's missing,'' Al said. His temper was closer to the surface than usual. Being queasy didn't help his disposition at all.

''I beg your pardon,'' Harding said, ''but you do not.'' He stood and stopped in front of Al, holding out his hands. ''These are not my hands even though, to me, they look like my hands. These belong to Dr. Samuel Beckett. For all intents and purposes, I *am*

Dr. Beckett. I look like him. I talk like him. I even understand physics. I could be him."

"You're not," Al said.

"Are you so certain?"

"Yes!" Al said. "To everyone else, you look like Sam. But to me, you look like a balding, middle-aged scientist who could afford to lose fifty pounds."

"And you are the only other one who has stood in the Imaging Chamber," Harding said.

"Are you saying that the Chamber has affected the Admiral's thought patterns?" Dr. Beeks asked. "Or are you saying that Dr. Beckett is manifesting a particularly diverse and colorful multiple personality disorder?"

"Manic-depression is a disease of the brain, Dr. Beeks," Harding said. "One that can be controlled with various drugs. Many other so-called mental disorders can be cured or controlled with medication. That suggests the brain is particularly vulnerable, like the body is vulnerable, to changes. Perhaps Dr. Beckett hasn't left at all. Perhaps this experiment has affected him in ways we do not yet understand."

"That would mean you're Sam," Al said.

"Yes," Harding said. "And you told me that Dr. Beckett was familiar with my work. You've been on the project a long time. I would wager you've seen photographs of me. I would think that—"

"I would think you should give us some credit," Ziggy said.

"Oh, I do. I think you're a marvelous computer," Harding said. "But that doesn't make you God, as you're claiming."

"She never claimed that," Al said, unable to believe he was defending Ziggy's ego.

"Ah, but she did," Harding said. "She is the only one who remembers the alternate time lines. She is the only one who knows why Dr. Beckett is Leaping."

"If she were God," Al said, "Sam would not be in this mess. She'd be able to bring him back."

"*If* he were actually gone." Harding leaned on the chair. "There have been studies—haven't there, Dr. Beeks?—to show that several personalities live within the brain. Stroke victims, for example, may suffer a complete personality shift. So may head injury victims."

"Dr. Beckett did not have a stroke," Dr. Beeks said.

"But we don't know what that Imaging Chamber does to the brain."

"You saw it," Al said. "You saw all the time lines I went through."

"And they were very general. Things a computer with a huge capacity could call up in an instant. No details of individual lives."

Dr. Beeks closed her eyes. She was standing beside Harding so he couldn't see her. Then she opened her eyes and shook her head just a little. "It's an interesting theory," she said finally. "But it is one we explored long before Project Starbright spent the first of its grant money."

"It's the only logical explanation," Harding said.

"For you, perhaps," she said. "You have a strong need for proof. I understand. You've come through quite a shock, and the admiral did take a tremendous risk explaining the Project to you. With that sort of informational overload, it is completely understandable that you would invent a scenario that would be the easiest for you.''

''Invent—?!'' Harding said.

''Invent,'' she said. ''You have spent a few hours on this project. The rest of us have spent years. You'll have to take us at our word on many things. Now, if you're willing to help us, you'll have to discard this theory, and work with another one.''

''Yeah,'' Al said. His dizziness was completely gone. ''Alternate realities. That discussion was triggering something for me. Every time we have trouble with changing time lines, Sam does something that directly affects the Project.''

''You brought Dr. Harding in,'' Dr. Beeks said. ''Perhaps you created some kind of paradox.''

Al shook his head. ''I brought Dr. Harding in after the change occurred. After Dr. Whatshername disappeared.''

''Dr. Fuller,'' Ziggy said. ''Samantha—Sammi Jo—Fuller.''

''Dixie Fuller?'' Harding sounded incredulous. ''She's a doctor?''

''A physicist,'' Ziggy said. ''Or she was, until something changed.''

''I didn't think that little girl had enough brain for simple multiplication,'' Harding said.

''Maybe you made her angry enough to prove you wrong, Dr. Harding,'' Dr. Beeks said sweetly.

''Until Dr. Beckett Leaped,'' Ziggy said in the same sweet tone as Dr. Beek's, ''Dr. Fuller was excelling in your field.''

''What's she doing now?'' Al asked, not wanting this thread to go on much longer. He was more interested in the Dr. Fuller of now.

"I don't know," Ziggy said a little too quickly. "I have lost track of her as well."

"No," Harding said. "She's with me. . . . Or, she was." He looked at them, his eyes wide. "In Loch Ness."

"Geez," Al said.

"We had already established that, Admiral," Ziggy said.

"I know!" Al patted the pockets of his suit coat for a cigar. "But you can't find her now, right?"

"Right," Ziggy said.

"What about in the past?"

"In the past, Admiral?"

"In Loch Ness, in 1986."

Ziggy was silent for a moment, but all the lights on her console flared. Multiple colors flashed like a disco from the midseventies. All they needed was a little Bee Gees and—

"I found her," Ziggy said. "Her brain patterns are as familiar as they always were."

"Great," Al said. "Center me on her, and send me there."

"It's not that easy, Admiral," Ziggy said.

Al shook his head. "And why not?"

"Because," Ziggy said. "She's in the eye of the time storm. In fact, I think she might be the eye."

"So?" Al asked.

"So," Ziggy said. "If you influence her in any way, the time stream will shift again. And we have no idea what that will do to Dr. Beckett."

CHAPTER SIXTEEN

If there is any primary rule of science, it is, in my opinion, acceptance of the obligation to acknowledge and describe all of reality, all that exists, everything that is the case. Before all else, science must be comprehensive and all-inclusive. It must accept within its jurisdiction even that which it cannot understand or explain, that for which no theory exists, that which cannot be measured, predicted, controlled, or ordered. It must accept even contradictions and illogicalities and mysteries, the vague, the ambiguous, the archaic, the unconscious, and all other aspects of existence that are difficult to communicate. At its best it's completely open and excludes nothing.

—ABRAHAM MASLOW, *THE PSYCHOLOGY OF SCIENCE*

Mount Shasta, California, Now.

The house was warm, and Sammi Jo had the shades drawn. She had no idea what time it was. She had heard the birds chirping outside a few hours ago and then they had stopped. She assumed that had been dawn.

She hadn't moved except to get herself breakfast. She had a bowl of Corn Pops balanced on her left knee, and she was staring at her screen. The phone numbers scrolled over it, changing color as the computer dialed them. She was eating absently, spooning food with her left hand, and using her right to execute an occasional keyboard command.

The computer had found its rhythm. It would dial and wait, sometimes getting a busy signal, sometimes getting a tone. The rapid, musical sound of the dialing was comforting. She could almost predict whether the machine would get a busy signal or a tone. It had been working for hours now, and hadn't yet received a voice communication. Sammi Jo had perused the list that Steve had given her. There were hundreds of numbers, but they all had the same area code and the same prefix. She had looked both of them up as she worked, and found they were all in Stallion's Gate, New Mexico.

Just like her ghost transmission.

The cereal tasted good, even though she had dribbled some of the milk down her leg. She had learned one nice thing about living in a resort town and having a bit of money: the grocery store delivered. She had had to disconnect the computer system for five minutes to call, but it had been worth the hassle. She now had enough food in the place to survive a nuclear winter.

If she should cause one.

She swallowed, the Corn Pops catching in her throat. Time travel, Steve had said. A think tank was desperate, Steve had said. So desperate that it would use illegal means to gain access to government research.

The whole thing terrified her. The think tank could be lying to Steve. Steve could be lying to her.

Or it could all be true.

Which explained that We-Missed-You message: it had come from the future.

Goosebumps rose on her skin. She set the bowl, still filled with milk, on the floor and wiped the drops off her bare calf. She hadn't been this desperate before.

As an adult, anyway. As an adult, she hadn't been this desperate. She remembered the feeling from her childhood, as clearly as if it were yesterday.

That strangled, caught-in-the-throat feeling, knowing that she had a secret but unable to remember it. Knowing she had been through something awful.

Screaming because she didn't want to go in the kitchen.

Screaming—

Screaming—

She closed her eyes, still seeing Leta Aider, tossing the flour canister off Sammi Jo's momma's neat sideboard, shattering the glassware, stopping at the knives. . . .

Sammi Jo opened her eyes, shivering. Sometimes she dreamed about that moment. If it was a good dream, she would end up in court, with her momma's lawyer, Larry Stanton, holding her, making her feel safe. And if it was a bad dream, Leta Aider would slash her own throat, then turn to Sammi Jo, the grin on her mouth matching the oozing grin in her neck, and she would come forward—

Sammi Jo stood up, knocking over the bowl. Milk ran through her socks and covered the hardwood floor, running along the tilt until it got to her dirty clothes pile. She grabbed a T-shirt off the top and wiped up the mess.

Travis used to be so interested in her past. He had wanted to meet her gramma, and when he finally did, he had had a long conversation with her. Or actually, a long monologue. Sammi Jo's gramma hadn't liked him, and she hadn't liked the questions he asked about Sammi Jo's father and Larry Stanton. When Travis finally left, Sammi Jo's gramma had said, "He'll never believe anything unless he has proof. He'll pretend to, but he won't. He's not for you, Samantha. He's not for you."

Her gramma had been right.

But Sammi Jo hadn't listened. Sammi Jo had spent so many years as the kid whose family was touched, the kid who saw Leta Aider kill herself, as that strange, smart little girl no one really liked.

So she had changed herself as best she could—she'd dumbed down her vocabulary, hid her smarts in every place except the classroom, and started calling herself Dixie. That had helped a little. It had given her a few friends.

It hadn't really cost anything either. She still had her dream, the one in which she would make something with her life. She somehow tied that dream to Larry Stanton, to the conversations she'd had with him when her momma was on trial. She had even, for a brief time in Loch Ness, thought about going back to school and majoring in physics. She knew she was smarter than Dr. Harding. She had thought it would be fun to prove to him how very smart she was.

Of course, that changed when Travis proposed. Over the years, Sammi Jo had come to realize that Travis had proposed just at that point because of his father's strange behavior, because of his father's rejection. But Sammi Jo had been needy herself at the time, and she hadn't seen that.

Or hadn't wanted to.

Sammi Jo wished her gramma were still alive so that she could talk to her. But she wasn't. She hadn't even made it to Sammi Jo's marriage to Travis. Sammi Jo's momma was living back East, and happily married, but Sammi Jo couldn't go to her. Pride wouldn't let her.

It had been hard enough telling her momma about the divorce.

I'd had such hopes for you, Sammi Jo, her momma had said.

Then her stepfather had added, *You know, you could still get into a good college if you wanted to.*

She hadn't wanted to. She still didn't want to. All she wanted was to be left alone, to figure out why her life had ended up this way, why no man had loved her, not her real father, and not Travis. She had always had to look elsewhere—to Larry Stanton, who had felt like a father to her, and who had left shortly after the trial, never to return—and to her stepfather, who still looked at her as a burden, part of the package he'd had to accept when he'd fallen in love with her momma.

At least her momma was happy.

At least one of them was.

A longer than normal silence caught her attention. She looked at the computer. A number was flashing red. The computer had dialed, but she wasn't getting a busy signal. She wasn't even getting a ring.

Something had already answered, and she had gotten a prompt. Then, before she could type anything, words scrolled across her screen:

DR. FULLER! YOU'RE BACK!

Her mouth was dry. She dropped the wet T-shirt beside her chair and sat back down.

DR. FULLER?

This was the moment. The moment Steve was paying her for. The moment the think tank wanted. If she didn't answer this prompt, they would never know. She would have their money, but she wouldn't have gone too far. She would still be in a gray area. An area where she could claim she had merely dialed the wrong number.

But if she answered, she was committed.

If she answered.

DR. FULLER?

She had studied that printout for weeks. This machine had used her name. It had known who she was.

She couldn't let that go. She would regret it for the rest of her life if she did.

Her hands shook as she reached for the keyboard. She eased her fingers onto the plastic keys and slowly typed:

I WAS NEVER GONE.

The cursor blinked silently. Perhaps she was breaking a code. Perhaps they were getting the authorities. She bit her lower lip and stared at the screen, hoping for a response, praying there wouldn't be one.

Praying there would be one.

The cursor continued to blink. She tightened her

right hand into a fist. Then, finally, words scrolled on her screen:

SAMMI JO! WHERE ARE YOU?

Her mouth was even drier than before. The remains of the milk tasted sour on her tongue. They had tried to trace her, had tried to track her down.

They had failed. So far.

She glanced at the box Steve had attached to her phone cable. Should she get the switch? Should she try to mislead them? Or did she need to?

Her heart was pounding so hard she thought the neighbors must be able to hear it. She got up. The floor was sticky under her bare feet. She hadn't wiped it well enough. She flipped one of the switches, more for her peace of mind than anything else, then went back to the computer.

SAMMI JO?

She sat down and typed:

HOW DO YOU KNOW MY NAME?

The gooseflesh pebbled on her arms. She had never seen a physical manifestation of fear like that before.

Only she wasn't consciously frightened. She felt disconnected from her body, as if her mind were a thing all its own, all by itself, floating free, free to concentrate on the problem before her.

I HAVE KNOWN YOU AS LONG AS YOU'VE KNOWN YOURSELF. WE MISS YOU, SAMMI JO.

She swallowed hard.

MISS ME? WHERE DID WE MEET?

The cursor blinked silently. She could almost feel the brain on the other end formulating an answer.

As a human being would do.

A shiver ran down her back. Then words appeared on the screen.

IN ANOTHER LIFETIME.

She frowned. Another lifetime. When she was married to Travis? Working in Silicon Valley? Was someone playing an elaborate joke on her?

A fifty-thousand-dollar joke?

Unlikely.

But still . . .

She ran a hand through her hair. She hadn't really looked at the money. She had noted that Steve had brought her mostly hundreds and several smaller bills, and that they were all the new treasury issue, the ones that, when they came out a few years back, reminded her more of Canadian money than U.S. currency.

It was supposed to be more difficult to counterfeit.

He wouldn't do that to her, would he?

Concentrate, she thought. She had to concentrate on the matter at hand.

WHO ARE YOU?

The response was immediate.

MY NAME IS ZIGGY. I'M A PARALLEL HYBRID COMPUTER.

She took her hands off the keyboard. A parallel hybrid computer? A hybrid of what? She had never heard of anything like that before, and she had worked very hard to remain current.

But then, Steve had said this project had to do with time travel, and it was secret government research. It would need computers.

Specialized computers.

I AM UNFAMILIAR WITH ANYTHING CALLED A PARALLEL HYBRID COMPUTER.

The screen blanked white, and for a moment she thought she had lost the connection. Then she checked her external modem and saw that the light was still on. She had a connection, but she wasn't certain if this Ziggy remained.

OF COURSE YOU'RE UNFAMILIAR WITH IT, DEAR. I'M A ONE OF A KIND.

"Sure," Sammi Jo muttered. "How convenient."

WHO CLAIMS TO KNOW ME?

Sammi Jo typed.

A few blips and numbers scrolled by too fast for her to catch.

Then words reappeared.

I "CLAIM" NOTHING, DEAR. I DO KNOW YOU. YOU'RE SAMANTHA JOSEPHINE FULLER, BORN MARCH 14, 1967, IN POTTERVILLE, LOUISIANA. YOUR MOTHER'S NAME IS ABAGAIL FULLER, YOUR FATHER OF RECORD IS WILL KINMAN. YOU GRADUATED FROM LINCOLN HIGH SCHOOL IN WHAT IS NOW A SUBURB OF CHICAGO, IL-

LINOIS. YOU MARRIED TRAVIS HARDING ON AUGUST 28, 1987, AND FILED FOR DIVORCE TWO WEEKS AGO.

Sammi Jo clenched her fists. *Think. Think.* She typed:

ALL OF THAT IS PUBLIC RECORD. YOU PROBABLY HAVE ACCESS TO ALL SORTS OF FILES.

Probably. So many doubts in that word.

OF COURSE I HAVE ACCESS. I HAVE ACCESS TO MORE INFORMATION THAN HUMANS CAN ABSORB IN A SINGLE LIFETIME, EVEN HUMANS WITH AN IQ OF 194.

Public records, Sammi Jo reminded herself.

The words continued to scroll:

BUT THAT DOESN'T TELL YOU HOW I KNOW YOUR NAME. YOU HAVEN'T IDENTIFIED YOURSELF, AND I DON'T KNOW WHERE YOU ARE.

Sammi Jo hoped not. If it did know where she was, this was an elaborate game and it was toying with her. Using her rental and phone records to obtain her name and then playing with her.

But that didn't explain the first contact. The one in Oakland before she left Travis. That had been on Steve's phone lines, in Steve's building. There had been no record of Sammi Jo then. She typed:

I ONLY HAVE YOUR WORD FOR THAT.

The cursor blinked for a half second.

MY WORD IS USUALLY GOOD ENOUGH.

Sammi Jo could almost hear the sniff of mock pain. The computer continued:

WELL, THEN, MAYBE THIS WILL HELP. YOUR GRANDMOTHER, LAURA FULLER, BELIEVED THAT A MAN NAMED SAM APPEARED WHENEVER YOUR MOTHER NEEDED HELP. YOUR GRANDMOTHER CLAIMED TO SEE THIS MAN, WHO DWELT IN THE BODIES OF THE PEOPLE WHO HELPED YOUR MOTHER. SHE CALLED HIM A WALK-IN. SHE ALSO SAW HIS COMPANION, AL, WHOM SHE DESCRIBED AS A GHOST.

Sammi Jo blinked back tears. She typed:

PUBLIC RECORD. MY GRANDMOTHER WAS INSTITUTIONALIZED.

The cursor blinked for a long time. Then it stopped. A single sentence appeared at once.

YOU WERE NEVER THIS CLOSE-MINDED IN YOUR PREVIOUS LIFE, SAMMI JO.

She shoved her chair away from the desk. For the first time, the room's darkness made her uncomfortable. Strange shapes lurked in the shadows. She was breathing hard. She couldn't separate from her body now. She had to think about this clearly. She had to focus, and she couldn't. This computer, this thing she was communicating with, seemed to know too much about her.

Finally, she stood over the keyboard and typed:

WHAT PREVIOUS LIFE?

THE ONE YOU WOULD HAVE HAD IF YOU HADN'T MARRIED TRAVIS HARDING.

The computer responded and then the screen went dead.

CHAPTER SEVENTEEN

> The child, the seed, the grain of corn,
> The acorn on the hill,
> Each for some separate end is born
> In season fit, and still
> Each must in strength arise to work the almighty will.
>
> —ROBERT LOUIS STEVENSON

Loch Ness, March 14, 1986.

Sam couldn't finish eating either. But he pushed the food around so that it looked like the three of them had made some sort of attempt. Mrs. Comyn had gone to some trouble and he didn't want to disappoint her, at least.

Sammi Jo.

The last time he had seen her, she had looked just like Abagail—the young Abagail—all wide-eyed and innocent, but with such a spark of intelligence that the touch of an idea could set her off. Innocent, intelligent, and sad.

I want to go back in time so I can tell my daddy . . .

Tell him what, honey?

Tell him that I love him.

Sam pushed away from the table. He put his napkin over his bowl, as Sammi Jo had done, and then he walked to the stairs. From above he could hear Travis, talking softly to Sammi Jo.

How Sam must have hurt her with that comment.

How he hadn't intended to.

He clenched his fist and put it over his heart. It wasn't fair. It wasn't fair that he had a daughter he could never talk to as a father. It wasn't fair that he didn't get to watch her grow up, to see how her mind worked, how she had managed to survive that awful past, how she had come to be here, with Travis.

It wasn't fair.

He had lost everything to do these Leaps. Why did he have to lose his child too?

Something was lodged in his throat. He swallowed, but was unable relieve the pressure. His daughter. Here. And it had taken him a while to recognize her. His Swiss-cheesed memory had cheated him of time here, as well as time with her growing up.

But that wasn't entirely true. He had recognized her.

Through the resemblance to Abagail.

He started up the stairs, and then he stopped. He didn't know how to deal with Sammi Jo yet. He didn't know how to talk to her as Donald Harding. He wanted to tell her everything. She was old enough to understand.

And Al was gone.

And if he told her everything, Sam might never go home.

But he might remain with his daughter.

He paused on the second step. This was too important to decide in a moment.

He turned around and went back through the hall. The water had stopped running down the stone, but a small puddle had formed against the wall. He passed it and went back into the public room.

It smelled of the hotchpotch. The dishes were still on the table, looking forlorn. He hurried past them and, pulling his slicker off the peg, went outside.

Night had fallen, accentuating the chill. The air felt damp and smelled of rain. A full moon had risen over the loch, appropriate, he thought, considering the events of the day.

He walked off the porch, across the stone steps, and down to the dock. The water lapped against the shore, making its own slapping sound against the rocks. Sam walked to the edge of the dock, his trail lit by moonlight, and sat cross-legged, staring at the water below.

He needed Al. That was all there was to it. Al would explain Sammi Jo's future to him, explain the risks, maybe even talk Sam out of the craziness he was thinking of.

He wanted to tell her.

He needed to tell her.

Of everyone he had known, she had the best capacity to understand. Strange things had happened throughout her life. She had a high IQ almost as high as his.

And she was wasting it with Travis.

Sam smiled. A fatherly thought at least, and not a thought Donald Harding would have. He would—and did—think that Travis was wasting his time with Sammi Jo.

What does Ziggy say I'm here for?

She doesn't know.

She doesn't—?

Well, she says there's a fifty percent chance that you're here to repair Harding's relationship with Travis.

Fifty percent. The lowest he had ever faced. Some of Ziggy's higher percentages had been wrong.

Some? Many.

He didn't know if it was possible to repair Harding's relationship with his son.

But Sammi Jo was here. And in the past, Sam had always Leaped to the right place and time to help Abagail. The last time he had done that, he had saved Sammi Jo, too.

From what?

He squinted, trying to remember. The light glinted off the loch, like sunlight on a cloudy day. The nights of the full moon were always so well lit, so magical.

Something splashed beside him.

He jumped and turned, half expecting to see a reptilian head, a humped back, a creature silhouetted against the gray sky.

Instead he saw Travis, moonlight full on the young man's face.

"Gotcha," Travis said. Then he grinned. " 'I do believe in ghosts. I do believe in ghosts. I do, I do. I do believe in ghosts.' "

He did a fair imitation of Bert Lahr as the Cowardly Lion.

"Ghosts, yes," Sam said, "but not a prehistoric creature trapped in a lake for centuries."

"Then why did you look when I threw that rock?"

Sam bit his lip, calculating the answer. "Maybe," he said, "maybe I want to believe."

"Why?" Travis asked. "You never have before."

"I never had to think about it before," Sam said. He stared out at the water. He loved the way the moonlight rippled with each movement. He could explain how light reflected and refracted; he could calculate how far they were from the moon based on the way light traveled. He could name the constellations they could see in this hemisphere, and if he tried, he could navigate by them.

But he couldn't see inside Travis's heart, any more than he could see inside Sammi Jo's, any more than he could explain to either of them that he was not Donald Harding, that he, in essence, was a ghost, just passing through their lives.

"You hurt Dixie," Travis said.

Sam turned away so that Travis couldn't see the pain on his face. "I didn't mean to."

"What were you asking her about? Why were you probing like that? To see if she's as wacko as I am?"

"No," Sam said.

"Then why?"

Sam took a deep breath. He had learned, on previous Leaps, that partial truths were better than complete fibs. "Because I think I've met her before."

"Where? In Chicago?"

"It doesn't matter," Sam said. "I was startled, that's all."

"And that's reason enough to hurt someone's feelings?"

Travis's words echoed across the water. On the other side, a mile away, someone was probably wondering who was arguing and why.

"No," Sam said quietly. "It's not." He rested his hands on his knees. The evening's chill reached through his sweater down to his skin. The last thing he wanted to do was alienate his daughter.

The last thing.

Travis sat down on the other side of the dock. Close to Sam, but not too close.

"You're different today," Travis said.

Sam couldn't count how many times he had heard that on Leaps. The one thing he couldn't change—he wouldn't change—was himself.

It was all he had.

"How so?"

"Calmer. More willing to listen. This morning, when you went off on that boat to prove to me that no such monster existed, that was you. But when you came back, you seemed different."

Travis had pinpointed the shift almost to the second. Sam was impressed. People had rarely done that before.

"It seemed tonight that when you asked Dix whether she'd ever believed her grandmother, you were being sincere."

"I was," Sam said.

"It's not like you." Travis drew his knees up to his chest. He rested his arms on top of them, and then put his chin on his wrists.

"I don't know," Sam said. "Asking questions is always at the root of knowledge."

"Dixie thinks you were asking just to be mean."

"I wasn't," Sam said. "Sometimes unreliable people speak the truth. I was only wondering if she'd thought of that."

"The truth about ghosts and walk-ins? Isn't that a bit harder terrain to cross than believing in a monster ten thousand people have seen?"

"Is it ten thousand?" Sam asked. "I had always thought it was a few."

"Thousands of documented sightings, Dad, and no, I won't let you change the subject."

Sam smiled to himself, glad Travis wasn't looking at him.

"Why'd you ask her that, Dad?"

His insides were quivering. And not with the cold. He couldn't explain it to Travis. No matter what. If he was going to talk to anyone, it would be Sammi Jo herself.

"Do you love her, Travis?" Sam asked.

"Why? You've never asked that about my other girlfriends."

So defensive. The relationship between Donald Harding and his son was obviously built on suspicion, accusation, and hurt. Deep, abiding hurt.

"I'm asking now," Sam said softly.

"You interested in her, Dad?"

The barb was sharp and unfair, and it landed, almost before Sam knew it had. He couldn't be interested, not in the way Travis was suggesting. The very thought appalled him. The idea that Travis would accuse his own father, seriously or not, of stealing his girlfriend offended him as well. Sam felt the heat rise in his face, the urge to get to his feet, but he forced himself to remain still, reminding himself that Travis wasn't angry at him, he was angry at Donald Harding, his father.

"No," Sam said. "I want to know how you feel about her."

He almost added, "Is that such a hard question to answer?" but didn't. Travis was difficult for anyone to get along with. He wondered why Sammi Jo had chosen him.

"Why?" Travis asked.

Sam took a deep breath. "Is my interest so unusual?"

"Frankly, yes, Dad."

Sam licked his lips. He didn't know how to ask the question. "You're clearly interested, but is it Sammi Jo or something else? I mean, you met at the tomb of a New Orleans voodoo priestess. She has all this strangeness in her past—"

"And you object, don't you? You want me to meet some normal scientist and settle down, have two-point-five geeky kids and a BMW, and maybe do some research that will feather your cap as well." Travis straightened out, his body tight as a wire. But he didn't get up.

"No," Sam said. "I was hoping you loved her, not all the mystery around her."

"What's the difference?" Travis asked, the bite out of his tone. He sounded genuinely curious.

Sam took a deep breath. He had to answer the question like Travis's father, not like Sammi Jo's. "Someday the mystery will go away, Trav."

Travis snorted. "Leave it to you to object to my girlfriend because she has a bit of the paranormal in her past." He stood. "I'm with her, Dad, because she understands me. Because she *wanted* to come to Scotland with me. She's looking for answers, just like I am, and she has an open mind. Which is more than I can say about you."

He started down the dock.

Sam didn't move. "Running away again?" he asked, keeping his voice even.

Travis stopped. "I'm not running away."

"Oh, yes, you are," Sam said. "Every time we reach a difficult point in the conversation, you accuse me of something and then run away. Whether we find the monster or not won't matter, Travis. Not if we can't have a discussion all the way to the end."

Travis didn't move. "If I stay, you'll just yell back at me."

"And if I promise I won't?"

"Then you'll shred me in that soft voice you're using now." Travis took a deep breath and turned. "Look, Dad, it was my idea to bring you here and I was wrong, okay? I don't need your help. I can raise the funds without you."

"I'm sure you can," Sam said softly. "But it wasn't your idea to come here this time. It was mine. I was at least willing to entertain the notion of helping you. And you might let me try."

Travis shook his head. "Hundreds of people come here every year, hoping to see the monster," he said, "and most of them never do. That's the thing about Nessie. She doesn't appear on command. I was a fool to think that once you saw the loch, once you felt the possibilities, you would understand. But that was my mistake. I forgot. You don't feel anything. You never have."

He stalked off the dock.

"See?" Sam said to the emptiness. "You run away." Then he sighed. No matter what he did, he couldn't seem to get through to Travis. Maybe Sam thought too much like Donald Harding.

Or maybe he didn't think enough like him.

But maybe, just maybe, that wasn't why Sam was

here. It seemed an odd coincidence that he was here and so was his daughter.

Was he here to aid her union with Travis? Or to prevent it?

Or was she in trouble in some other way?

The only way he could find out was to ask. Which meant he needed to talk to her, and he had to do so without alienating her, something that would be difficult, given his relationship—Harding's relationship—with Travis.

Out in the moonlit water, something splashed. Sam looked up in time to see the water spout in a geyser and splatter across the surface. Ripples formed all the way to the shore, slapping the water against the rocks. The moonlight sparkled on an empty lake.

"Fish," he mumbled. "Just fish jumping."

But for a moment, he wasn't so sure.

CHAPTER EIGHTEEN

When you investigate something, you change the nature of what you investigate. Impossible to intervene without altering reality. Physicists know that well enough; they call it indeterminancy.

—IAN WATSON, *MIRACLE VISITORS*

Stallion's Gate, New Mexico, Now.

Al took a deep breath, then snatched the Saltines from Gooshie. Ziggy's comment had upset Al more than he was willing to admit. Why weren't these things ever easy?

No one had moved. Ziggy's lights still strobed, but everything else remained the same. The chair sat forlornly to one side. Dr. Beeks stood close to Donald Harding, as if she were protecting him. Tina glanced over her shoulder at Al, then went back to work on Ziggy's console. Gooshie opened his hands, displaying his palms, as if he were not to blame for the sharpness of Al's movements. Ziggy was uncharacteristically silent, although her blinking lights continued the room's disco effect.

Al ate a few more crackers, wishing for a cigar,

knowing that putting something in his mouth in times of stress was a learned reaction but one he wasn't willing to change.

"If we go to this Samantha Fuller," he said as calmly as he could, "we might find Sam."

"Or we might lose him forever," Ziggy said.

"It seems that you have lost him already," Harding said. "And as fascinating as I find this, I would like to return to my own life."

"Would you now?" Al turned, clutching the box of Saltines. "You look on all this as one big game, don't you, Doctor? You've never met Sam Beckett. You don't understand the stakes we're working on here."

"Admiral," Dr. Beeks warned.

Al waved her away. He'd already brought Harding into this. He may as well give the guy all the information. "This isn't a sabbatical, Doctor, nor is it a trip to a secret government research lab, one you can take a vow of silence about and then return to your world."

"Admiral," Dr. Beeks said again.

"If we fail, you can go anywhere you want. You can do anything you want. But if you claim to be Donald Harding, people will look at you oddly. You'll spend the rest of your life as Dr. Sam Beckett. Your kid won't know you, your colleagues won't believe you, and your career will be over. You'll have to step into Dr. Beckett's shoes, and frankly—"

"Admiral!" Dr. Beeks snapped.

"And frankly," Al said loudly to cover the sound of her voice, "you could never fill them. No one could."

He sank down in the chair someone had pulled for Harding, clutching the box of Saltines to his chest as if it were a small child. The risk was his call. The whole thing was his call. If they went back, focusing on Whatshername's brain patterns, and lost Sam, it would be on Al's head.

"Admiral," Ziggy said softly, in a wheedling voice, a voice that made chills run up his spine.

He clutched the Saltines box tighter and closed his eyes. "It better be good news, Ziggy."

"Good, bad, all depends on your perspective, Admiral." She actually had a shrug in her tone. An I-don't-care-how-you-take-it shrug, an I'm-just-the-messenger shrug. Why couldn't she have a flat voice, an elevator voice, like all the computers in the movies?

Except HAL, from the movie *2001*. HAL had a warm, wheedling voice, a seductive voice.

"Admiral?" Ziggy asked.

He leaned his head back. His mouth was dry from the Saltines. "Tell me the news," he said, preparing himself for the worst.

"I have located Sammi Jo Fuller. Now."

"Now." His eyes snapped open. He sat up, feeling woozy and strange and oddly nervous. "Today? This minute?"

"Yes," Ziggy said.

"Where is she?"

"I have been talking to her through one of the emergency phone links Dr. Beckett set up."

"What emergency phone link?" Tina asked. She had a hand on one shapely hip, and Al recognized that look. Her eyes had narrowed, her mouth was thin. She was one of Ziggy's technicians. She should know about any emergency phone links, and she didn't know about this.

Al stood up. He always felt better on his feet when Tina was pissed. "I haven't heard of any, Tina," he said.

"Dr. Beckett set up several back doors into my system so that he could access information without a handlink and without coming here. The system was designed for any and all emergencies he could think of, except, of course, the one we've experienced since the Project started."

"Of course," Gooshie murmured.

Tina crossed her arms. "How are you talking to her?" she asked.

"On-line. She found the back door herself. I have broken off communications for the moment, but left the line open."

"Where is she?" Al asked. "*What* is she?"

"She is . . . divorced." The faint pause before the word "divorce" told Al that Ziggy knew a story behind that relationship, a story she didn't want to share at the moment. "She's living in Mount Shasta, California, running illegal computer programs for . . . a friend."

"Illegal?" Al asked. "And we had her working here?"

"In a different time line, Admiral. In this time line, she never went to college. She married young and . . . got sidetracked."

"What are you keeping from us on this, computer?" Harding asked. "You sound as if you don't want us to know all the facts."

"I could, Admiral," Ziggy said, ignoring Harding,

"ask her if she remembers Dr. Harding's presence in Loch Ness."

"But I was there," Harding said. "It would do no good."

"And ask if he exhibited some sort of personality change. It might help."

"It couldn't hurt," Tina said. "Ask."

"Wait," Al said. He set the Saltines box on the control panel. Gooshie snatched the box off and set it on the floor. "What'll that prove?"

"It will give us some hope that Dr. Beckett is still in Loch Ness," Ziggy said.

"And how do we get to him?" Gooshie asked.

Al took a deep breath. He finally knew what Ziggy was getting at. "It means if we have at least some evidence that Sam was there, and then we lock onto Sammi Jo Fuller's brain patterns in 1986, we'll be taking a calculated risk by sending me there. A smart gamble."

"That's an oxymoron if I ever heard one," Dr. Beeks muttered.

"At least there'd be a chance I could hook up with Sam, and we could discover what he's changed and set it right."

"It has something to do with me," Harding said. "Something he didn't do that I did."

"Or vice versa," Al said.

"Or something that he's continuing to do," Tina said. "That would explain why there's a time storm around this Fuller girl."

"What did you think of her, Doctor?" Dr. Beeks asked.

Harding shrugged. "I didn't pay a lot of attention to her. She seemed rather waiflike and calf-eyed. She had some sort of trauma in her past, and she mixed it up with ghosts. I was afraid Travis had hooked up with her because she needed protecting. I really didn't care for the fact that my son was with a girl who had the IQ of a dead chipmunk."

"She has an IQ of 194, Doctor," Ziggy said, "which is sixty points higher than yours and fifty-five higher than your son's."

Al slapped Ziggy's console. "Atta girl," he mumbled under his breath.

But Dr. Beeks was frowning. "He ignored her," she said.

"Dr. Beckett would never ignore anyone," Gooshie said.

"He would if she wasn't good enough for his kid," Harding said, a bit defensively.

"She's more than good enough," Al said. Something was niggling at his brain. Something from a previous Leap. "Sammi Jo Fuller. Samantha Fuller. Ziggy, wasn't she—?"

"Abagail Fuller's daughter, yes," Ziggy said.

And then it all came back to Al. Or at least, those three rapid Leaps, the ones in which Sam got entangled with Abagail Fuller, and she gave birth to a daughter named Sammi Jo, a daughter Ziggy said had a 91.9 percent chance of being Sam's daughter as well.

"But I thought Sam's Leap as Larry Stanton saved her from working on computer manuals in a trailer park."

"It did," Ziggy said. "She's not doing that. She was working here, and now she's not. But she never wrote computer manuals, and she never lived in a trailer park. She married—well."

"Instead she's a hacker," Harding said. "I knew she'd come to a bad end."

"It's interesting that Dr. Beckett would cause her to come to a grief," Gooshie said. "That's not usually how it works."

"Unless he changed something just by his arrival," Tina said.

"Possible," Al said. "We gotta get me back there, Ziggy. Talk to the girl, find out what happened, then send me to Loch Ness."

"All right, Admiral," Ziggy said. "But I have to warn you that this may not work."

Al nodded. He was fully aware of that. But right now, it was the best shot they had.

CHAPTER NINETEEN

I refuse to believe that God plays dice with the universe.

—ALBERT EINSTEIN

Mount Shasta, California, Now.

Sammi Jo was pacing. She didn't want to break the telephone connection, but she didn't want to get caught. She knew that if she lost the connection this time, it would disappear, maybe for good.

Another lifetime.

One in which she did not marry Travis Harding.

Life without Travis.

It felt right.

It felt wrong.

She wouldn't be the same person without him. She certainly wouldn't be sitting here, with fifty thousand dollars in cash and a moral dilemma that was eating her up inside.

She hadn't typed a response yet. Maybe if she did, the computer would come back. But it hadn't left a prompt for her. It had just disappeared.

Like a ghost.

She rubbed her hands over her arms. They were ribbed with gooseflesh. She stopped and adjusted the heat. It was cold outside, even though the sun was out. That's what she got for moving to the mountains. A chill, even this late in the season.

A chill. Like someone had walked on her grave.

If she hadn't married Travis Harding . . . If she hadn't married Travis Harding, what would she have done? If she hadn't met him, she would have gone home alone from her trip to New Orleans. Not home to Chicago, but home to Louisiana, to confront the ghosts of her past. As it was, she went back with Travis and the experience was completely different. She explained her past to him at each landmark, from the hanging tree where her mother had nearly died, to the well into which Violet Aider had fallen, to the courtroom where Larry Stanton had saved her mother from prison. They had avoided the house where Sammi Jo had grown up, and where Leta Aider had killed herself in a fit of desperate rage.

The house, which had been Sammi Jo's original destination. She had planned to face it once and for all. When the time came, though, she had felt that she didn't need to, not with Travis beside her. With Travis beside her, she could move on in her life without stopping to bury old demons.

And she had. That tour of New England's haunted houses, the trip to Loch Ness, where Travis proposed. Then came all the rest of the psychics' must-see stops in Europe. She had thought herself richer, more fulfilled for all of those.

And she married Travis after them.

And then they had stayed in the States, while he pursued his studies. While she began to realize that he had a talent for finding the charlatan, for ripping off the public, for using his scientific upbringing to give legitimacy to his increasingly shady enterprises.

In a different life, she had worked with a parallel hybrid computer. That would have required education, right? Something she had never had.

Something she had once planned on.

She closed her eyes and swallowed. It must all be an elaborate ruse. Steve had come into money somehow, and he'd established all of this to help her get on her feet.

Her stomach felt hollow. He had never been that good a friend. Maybe he was testing her, seeing how woo-woo she really was before giving her the next project.

But fifty thousand dollars. A man didn't toss around fifty thousand dollars as a test.

The room smelled of sour milk, and she was hungry. She went into the kitchen, opened a box of Triscuits and a can of Diet Coke, and carried them back to the computer.

The cursor was blinking again.

After a prompt.

The computer—or whatever it was—had returned.

She had had enough. She sat down at her keyboard and tapped out her question:

WHAT KIND OF GAME IS THIS?

The response was instantaneous.

IT IS NOT A GAME. YOU CONTACTED ME, REMEMBER?

So she had. But not without help.

YOUR NUMBER WAS GIVEN TO ME.

The computer's responses were lightning fast, much faster than they had been before. As if it were concentrating all its energy on her now.

THEN YOU MUST CONTACT THAT PERSON ABOUT THE "GAME," NOT ME. UNTIL THEN, THOUGH, I WOULD LIKE YOU TO ANSWER SOME QUESTIONS.

"I bet you would," Sammi Jo muttered. The computer didn't wait for her answer.

WHEN YOU WERE IN LOCH NESS IN 1986, DO YOU REMEMBER A DONALD HARDING?

She stared at the screen. Why wouldn't she remember Donald Harding? He was her father-in-law. Or rather, ex-father-in-law.

I MET DONALD HARDING IN CUPERTINO, CALIFORNIA.

The computer didn't hesitate.

SO YOU DID. I MISPHRASED. DO YOU REMEMBER DONALD HARDING ACCOMPANYING YOU AND TRAVIS HARDING ON YOUR LOCH NESS TRIP IN 1986?

The trip that had happened over her birthday. The trip that was supposed to fund their monster research and had, instead, caused the last breach between father and son.

Except . . .

She put a hand to her forehead. Donald Harding had contacted Travis a year ago. Something about breakthrough research. Something that they both could share. Donald's think tank was investigating—

Time travel.

She flushed. Suddenly all of this was making sense. She put a hand over her mouth so that she wouldn't type anything rash. The biggest problem with on-line communication was typing rash things.

Donald Harding had a think tank involved in time travel.

Travis Harding had filed for divorce against his wife, whom, he knew, occasionally dabbled in illegal computer activities for a guy named Steve.

Father and son couldn't have conspired to put her in a bad position so that they would improve Travis's position in the divorce, could they? She hadn't asked for anything.

She had used the money her mother had sent to hire a lawyer, and the lawyer had mumbled something about community property laws. She would be entitled to half of Travis's earnings during their marriage and continued earnings for anything he had developed during that marriage.

Including the very profitable psychic hotline.

Sammi Jo had promised to think about it, and she'd promptly forgotten it. In fact, she had only just written to her attorney to notify her of the change of address.

But the attorney was acting for her. Travis knew that. The billable hours were probably stacking up.

The Diet Coke churned in her stomach. If the attorney had once mentioned community property, then Travis would have gone into a panic.

But enough of a panic to conspire with his father? His father, whom he'd vowed to hate for life?

She brought her hand down from her mouth. Her

fingers were shaking. She had already made the connection, already committed the illegal act. Terminating it now wouldn't make a difference, would it?

It would.

Slowly she reached up and hit the macro for her dial service hang-up. A series of numbers scrolled across the bottom of the screen. She captured the conversation, printed it, and then shut off her machine.

Her hands hadn't stopped shaking.

She reached into the dirty laundry, felt the book bag full of cash, and knew how it would look if and when the police arrived. What to do? What to do?

The best thing was to get it out of the house. If she remembered correctly, the police needed a warrant to open someone's safe-deposit box. And for that they would have to know that the person actually had a box.

She could open a box and throw away the key.

Or hide the key. That would be much easier than hiding a wad of cash.

She slung the book bag over her shoulder, grabbed her car keys, and left the house. She pulled the locked door closed behind her, wishing suddenly she had a better security system.

The light was gray and diffuse. The mountain looked powerful and threatening, the chill in the air seemed to flow from the snowy peak. What had ever possessed her to live near a volcano?

She got in her ancient, battered Volkswagen Rabbit and slid the book bag under the seat. She sat for a moment, uncertain as to where to go. They'd look in the Shasta banks first.

But no one knew her in Redding. It was only a few hours away.

The clock on the dashboard showed it was nearing ten in the morning. She had time.

She hoped.

CHAPTER TWENTY

Two things stand like stone:
Kindness in another's trouble,
Courage in your own
—ADAM LINDSAY GORDON

Loch Ness, March 14–15, 1986.

She was waiting for him when he went in, standing before the fire Mrs. Comyn had made, twisting her hands—wringing them as if they were wet laundry. Sam had never seen anyone do that before.

The table behind her had been cleared off, and the room straightened. The faint smell of hotchpotch still hovered in the air.

He held the door open a moment and gazed at her, his daughter, looking frail and strong and stubborn all at the same time. Abagail had the same stance, all courage, conviction, and vulnerability mixed up in one.

Sammi Jo had gotten so much from her mother, and so little from him.

Time had conspired against them, and she didn't even know it.

He let the door close loudly. It banged in the public room, making Sammi Jo jump. The fire provided the only light, making the wood amber, giving the room a feel of a sepia photograph. He felt, somehow, as if he had stepped into a very ancient past, a past not his own.

Which, he supposed, was accurate.

Except for the ancient part.

He took off his slicker and hung it near the door. Then he came in, stopping near one of the tables.

"Sammi Jo," he said.

"Dixie," she corrected.

"Dixie," he said softly, hoping she wouldn't take offense. His heart was pounding. He hadn't felt this way since—since—well, since he had seen her when she was a child. Years ago for her, a skip in time for him.

"I was waiting for you," she said. She hadn't turned to look at him. She hadn't moved at all.

He didn't know what to ask. He didn't know how to play the role of Donald Harding. He didn't think he could.

"Travis says you didn't mean to insult me." She held out her hands, as if warming them over the fire. "I can believe that. I take offense easy on things like that."

"I'm sorry," Sam said.

She nodded, acknowledging his words without really giving him credit for them. "He says you think we met before. We never met before."

The certainty in her voice chilled him. It was now or never. He grabbed a chair and pulled it to the fire. Then he grabbed another. He held out his hand.

"Sit," he said. She looked at the offered chair but didn't move. "Please."

Finally she did, with the ease and gracefulness of a princess.

"What do you know of physics?"

"Don't make fun of me, Dr. Harding. You know I only went to high school."

Sam sat across from her. He put his hands on his knees, trying to look sympathetic, fatherly, and relaxed. "I'm not mocking you, Sammi Jo. Dixie. I'm not trying to patronize you either. But I do want to have a conversation with you."

She took a deep breath. "I never had much physics. A bit of chemistry, lots of biology, but not much physics. You need math for that, and I never got past Advanced Algebra."

"Why not?"

She smiled, ducking her head, embarrassed. "Mr. Figgs, our algebra teacher, he liked to write problems on the board. I corrected him a few times. So one day, he asked me to do a problem in front of the class, and as I did, he fixed every chalk stroke, erased and wrote over every line."

"He shamed you."

"He made it clear no little girl, 'specially a dumb little Southern girl named Dixie, should question him."

"But he was only one teacher," Sam said.

"I went to a small high school, Dr. Harding. He was the only math teacher, and I woulda had to have him for precalc and calc. I couldn't face two more years of him."

The fire made the room hot. It smelled of wood smoke. "What about college?" he asked.

She pushed off the chair. "I knew you was gonna ask about that. Am I not smart enough for Travis? Is that it? You want some pretty girl with an IQ off the charts?"

"Like yours?" Sam asked.

She froze.

"One hundred ninety-four, if I remember right," Sam said, "and I usually do. I have a photographic memory. Seems to me that you do too."

She wrapped her arms around herself, as if she were hugging herself. "What do you want, Dr. Harding?"

"I want to talk to you," he said. "I want to know your capacity for belief. To believe impossible things."

"Like the monster?" Her smile was bitter.

"No," he said. "Things like your grandmother said."

"My gramma was in an asylum." Sammi Jo said that as if the sentence were rote, as if that were the explanation for a thousand problems she had faced in her life.

"So are a lot of people. That doesn't mean they can't speak the truth."

"Why are you diggin' into that, Dr. Harding? 'Coz it's so unusual? Or 'coz you think Travis is interested in me 'coz of that?"

Sam bit his lip. Beside him, the fire cracked and sparks flew. The heat in the room was growing unbearable. "Travis told you that."

"We don't hold secrets from each other." She gripped herself tighter.

Maybe he shouldn't tell her. Maybe he should just let her be. But he couldn't. Not this time. He didn't have a compelling reason to remain silent. When he was Larry Stanton, he had had to be silent. He'd had to save Abagail.

Abagail was fine now. Sammi Jo had said so.

"Do you remember, when you were eleven, talking with Larry Stanton, your mother's attorney?"

She brought her chin up. Her face was in profile in the firelight. "What of it?"

"You told him that your favorite book was *Brigadoon*. He said his was too. He even gave you a copy of the book."

"So?" she said.

"Then you told him you wanted to go back in time. You wanted—" Sam felt a lump in his throat. He forced himself to swallow. "You wanted to see your father, to tell him you loved him."

"What do you want, Dr. Harding?"

Sam closed his eyes, took a deep breath. Courage. If he was going to tell her, he had to do it now. "What if I told you that my real name is Sam Beckett, that I was Larry Stanton during your mother's murder trial, and Will Kinman in the days before you were born, and your grandfather Clayton Fuller the night he saved your mother from the burning house? What if I told you that I travel through time, and somehow I'm drawn to places where you are, where your mother is? What if I told you I am your—"

"Stop it! Stop it now!" She wasn't yelling. It was somehow worse because she wasn't yelling. Her arms had fallen to her sides, and her fists were clenched. "Travis said you was mean, but I didn't know how mean. He said you had this mocking cruel side that went so deep no one could get past it. If you want to break me and Travis up by bein' nasty to me, it won't work. It won't. I'll love him no matter what you do."

A light sweat had broken out all over Sam's body. He had blown it. He'd had one chance, and he had blown it.

"I'm not trying to break you up," Sam said. "I'm trying to talk to you. Give me one chance, Sammi Jo. Just one. For one minute, and then you can be mad."

"No," she said. "I won't let you mock me. My gramma's Sam was her white knight, not mine. You can't use it. I loved her despite her problems, and I love my momma still."

"Your mother believes in this Sam?" He couldn't keep the need out of his voice.

She swallowed. He could see her delicate Adam's apple move. She held her head rigid. "She says my daddy was never the same after he saved her. But that coulda been stress. Lord knows people change after serious events. There's been all kinda studies on that."

"There have," Sam said. "And there've also been times when unexplained things happened. You never told me about your conversations with Larry Stanton—"

"Well, someone did." Her eyes were reflecting the firelight. It took him a moment to realize they were swimming with tears.

"Physics, Sammi Jo," he said softly. At least she hadn't run away yet. "Remember how this started?"

"I told you I never had physics. That makes it easy for you. You can use my ignorance to make up some kinda strange story about how a weird branch of physics created the walk-ins my gramma believed in."

Sam tried not to groan. When a powerful mind refused to believe something, it refused hard. "What kind of proof do you need?" he asked.

Her lower lip trembled. "I don't need proof," she said. "I need you to stop playing this game. I need you to stop."

"I'm not playing a game, Sammi Jo."

She clenched her fist, looked away from him into the fire. The light on her face aged it, brought out the resemblance to Abagail, the last time he had seen her.

When he couldn't touch her.

It was amazing how much he loved that woman, and how proud he was of this daughter, this child of a Leap.

He was breaking all the rules. He had to let it go. Had to.

"If you're telling the truth," she said, "why haven't you said anything before?"

"I just arrived this morning, Sammi Jo."

"On the boat," she whispered.

"On the boat," he said.

"I thought, when people traveled in time, they did it in their own bodies."

He nodded. "That's how fiction does it. But it doesn't work that way, at least for me. I—we—call it Leaping and I seem to appear in people's lives to solve a problem, and then I disappear, never managing to stay long."

"It's a fantastic idea." Her voice was cool. "What do physics gotta do with it?"

"It's how we devised the system, through a branch of physics called quantum mechanics."

"Dr. Harding's specialty," she said, and the mocking tone had returned to her voice. "How convenient."

Sam swallowed. "Dr. Harding's research had a major influence on my work," he said.

"I'm sure it did." She smiled at him, the smile weak, trembly, and insincere. "Nice try, Doctor, but it won't work. It's too easy. You see, to make an accurate test of a person's ability to believe in the impossible, you need to make the impossible plausible."

"Like a monster in a freshwater lake, a monster that has been there for generations."

"Actually," she said, "people believe a family of monsters lives in Loch Ness. The loch is deep and cold, and them monsters could survive down there, breedin'. No one knows how long they live, but the sightings have happened since 565 A.D. That's a long time, long enough for the creatures to have developed their own community, to have achieved a sort of life away from their normal grounds."

"You find this plausible, but not what I'm saying?"

She smoothed her hair back with one hand. "Dr. Harding, I told you about my gramma at dinner. Then tonight you come back with this story. Maybe, maybe if you had told me this morning, when you'd come off that boat, I mighta believed you. Although I doubt it. Travis has been fascinated with my family from the moment he heard about them. Sometimes I think he's as interested in them as he is in me. And I think that's all right. I'd rather have him interested than frightened."

"Are most people frightened?" Sam asked.

"Why wouldn't they be? My gramma is in an asylum. My momma was accused of murder. And then there's me, the scrawny little girl with the big brain who asks too many questions and knows too much. At least until Dixie. You said to me once that I was too quiet. You thought I wasn't very smart 'coz of the way I talked and 'coz I was so quiet. You're wrong, Dr. Harding. I'm quiet 'coz I learned that it's best to keep your thoughts and opinions to yourself. I talk like this 'coz it's what people expect. They aren't so threatened by a good ole Southern girl named Dixie. But smart little girls, especially ones who test off the charts, blow all the stereotypes. That math teacher, he was common. I had other teachers try to slow me down, try to stop me from getting ahead of the class. My seventh-grade reading teacher gave me Cs just so that I would know what it felt like."

Sam swallowed. He had never experienced anything like that, growing up smart in Indiana. All he had received was encouragement. But his sister had quit math because, she'd claimed, it bored her.

"What about gifted programs?" he asked.

She snorted. "They didn't have gifted programs in the seventies, at least not at small schools, especially not in the South."

"I thought you moved to Chicago," he said.

"Near Chicago." She shook her head. "The gifted programs near me was all private. We couldn't afford that."

"No," he said, wishing he had been there, wishing he had been able to help. "I suppose you couldn't. But that's no reason to give up."

"Give up, Dr. Harding? Who says I gave up?"

"On yourself. On your education."

"Do you know how much it costs to go to college?"

He nodded. "It's always been expensive. But there are scholarship programs, loans offers. Some of the good schools aren't as expensive as the others—"

"I didn't get no scholarship," she said.

"Did you take your SAT?"

"No." She stood. "What is this? The fifth degree? Will you like me if I have an education, Dr. Harding? Or are you trying to corrupt me, to teach Travis that his is the way of ignorance?"

"I already approve of you, Sammi Jo," Sam said. "Whatever you choose to do."

She froze. Her hand gripped the side of her chair. Then she stood, slowly. "I hope you're not just saying that," she said softly. "I pray God you're not just saying that."

"I mean it," he said.

She looked at him. Her eyes were wide, her nose red. For the first time, he no longer saw himself or Abagail in her, but he saw that little girl in her, the one who had sobbed her way through the tale of a horrible suicide, and who had saved her mother's life.

"If you do mean it," she said, "then you can stop testing me. No more lies about walk-ins, no more attempts to become buddy-buddy with me using my own past."

"I promise," he whispered, feeling a deep and sudden ache in his heart.

"And promise me you'll work with Travis on his idea. Your reputation should not be more important than your relationship with your son."

"It shouldn't, shouldn't it?" Sam said.

She crossed her arms and smiled at him. It was a real smile this time. "You should be like this more often, Dr. Harding. People might actually get along with you.''

''And you should stand up for yourself more often, Sammi Jo,'' he said.

She nodded, and for the first time since he'd Leaped here, he felt as if he had taken the first steps toward an understanding.

CHAPTER TWENTY-ONE

> Man seems to have no function except that of dissipating or degrading energy.
>
> —HENRY ADAMS

Stallion's Gate, New Mexico, Now.

"She broke the connection, Admiral." Ziggy's voice echoed in the high-ceilinged space. Al chomped on the cigar he had gotten from his stash in his room near the lab. He was glad for it. The cigar, more than anything, had settled his stomach.

"She hung up?" Gooshie asked. He was bent over the console, studying the readouts. Tina was beside him.

"Yes," Ziggy said.

"But we know where she is," Tina said.

"Why would she break the connection?" Al asked. "The questions were harmless."

"She seemed uneasy when I mentioned Dr. Harding," Ziggy said. "She never answered my questions about him."

Al turned to Harding. The man was leaning against the wall, arms crossed over his ample stomach. His skin was flushed and his small eyes intense.

"What did you do to her, you nozzle?" Al asked.

Harding shrugged. "It's your mysterious Dr. Beckett who is there with her, not me."

"Admiral," Ziggy said, a caution in her voice. "I need to speak to you alone."

Al pulled the cigar out of his mouth so that he wouldn't bite the end off it. He pointed the cigar at Harding. "You shouldn't be standing around anyway. Gooshie, take this guy into one of the research rooms, and get him working on all the information we have about time storms, paradoxes, and the experiment. I planned to use this hundred-pound brain, and he's standing around pretending the experiment doesn't even exist."

"That might be how he copes, Admiral," Dr. Beeks said.

"I don't have time for coping," Al said. "We need results. Now, the rest of you, clear out and leave me with Her Royal Smartness."

Gooshie glanced at Tina, who was suppressing a smile. Then Gooshie came over and took Harding's arm. Harding shrugged him off, but together they left the room. Dr. Beeks followed. Tina hesitated a moment.

"You go on too, sweetheart," Al said.

"You could use my help," she said.

"Probably, but Ziggy here wants to have a discussion *mano a mano*. I'm not going to argue."

Tina smiled and let herself out of the room. Al was alone with the biggest, smartest computer in the country, probably in the world. And she seemed humble for once.

"Admiral, I'm not sure how much you remember about Sammi Jo Fuller—"

"Nothing about her stay here," he said, putting the cigar back in his mouth. "But I got the whole conception, murder-trial thing firmly in mind."

"Good," Ziggy said. "She was in Loch Ness, as we know, and sometime after that, she married Travis Harding."

"If he's anything like dear ole Dad, she was smart divorcing the dweeb."

"That's the point," Ziggy said. "Donald Harding is her father-in-law, and the divorce involves a lot of money. She might think he's involved in some way, that my communication with her has something to do with him and his son."

"Ah, geez," Al said. If there was anything he understood, it was divorce. "And we have the wrong Donald Harding here because he doesn't understand any of this."

"Exactly, Admiral."

Al paced for a moment. The room seemed cavernous without the others in it. And he had never really liked the colors. They were too tame for him. Even with the flashing lights.

Although those had stopped.

"How did you find her?" Al asked.

"Actually, Admiral, she found me. She accidentally tapped our lines—"

"I thought you said she was doing illegal work for a friend," Al said, stopping and putting a hand to his forehead. He was getting a headache. Or an idea. Sometimes they felt like the same thing.

"She was, Admiral."

"So she hacked her way into your data banks. Illegally."

"Technically," Ziggy said. She had an odd reluctance in her voice. Could it be that Ziggy was fond of Samantha Josephine Fuller? Was Ziggy fond of anyone besides Sam?

"Technically is all we need," Al said. "In fact, it's perfect."

"Perfect?"

"She broke the law. We have a legitimate excuse to use federal resources to find her. We bring her here, we ask her questions, and she can't leave until she's answered them. Then we can send me back to Sam."

"Perhaps," Ziggy said. "But then we would have another problem."

Al wasn't certain how many more problems his mind could take. "What's that, Ziggy, old girl?"

"Sammi Jo Fuller is, in all statistical likelihood, Dr. Beckett's daughter."

"Yes?"

"Which means she shares his DNA."

"Yes?"

"If we link you to her, Admiral, she might be able to see you."

"Like Sam can."

"Yes, Admiral. And unlike the chances you are taking with Dr. Harding, if you succeed in going back to Loch Ness with the help of Sammi Jo Fuller, if you succeed, Admiral, she will remember you."

Al put his cigar back in his mouth. "That won't be so bad, will it, Ziggy?"

"It will change the future again, Admiral. She may not marry Travis Harding, but she may not come back here either."

Al frowned. "How important is her return?" he asked. "Provided, of course, we can get her into a better situation than she is in now, I mean."

"How important?" Ziggy said. "Let me put it to you delicately, Admiral. I have run all the statistical models I can. If Sammi Jo Fuller sees you, and does not return to the lab, she still has a good chance at an excellent future. It is not her that I'm worried about in this case. It's Dr. Beckett."

"Why?" Al asked.

"Because," Ziggy said. "All the models show that there is an eighty-five percent chance that the person who finds Dr. Beckett's route home is none other than his daughter. She can't help him if she's not at the lab."

Al closed his eyes. "Oh, boy," he whispered.

CHAPTER TWENTY-TWO

The deil's bairns hae ay the deil's luck.
—SCOTTISH PROVERB

Mount Shasta, California, Now.

Sammi Jo had three errands to do before she left Mount Shasta City, and she couldn't avoid any of them. First, she returned briefly to the house and wrote e-mail to Steve, withdrawing from his project and telling him that she would return the fee. Then she went to the bank and withdrew fifty dollars, hoping, praying it would be enough to get her to Redding and back. Finally, she stopped at the local Texaco and filled her Rabbit with gas. She checked the oil, washed the windshield, and added fluids. When the attendant insisted on helping her, she let him, not wanting to draw any more attention to herself than necessary. When he asked if she was just passing through, she smiled at him vaguely, as if she hadn't heard him, and went inside to pay.

It was a beautiful sunny afternoon. The sky was blue, the mountain a looming presence. She did love it here, and she wasn't certain how she could stay.

She wasn't certain how she would survive without Steve's money. But she had to try.

Even if it meant borrowing some cash from her folks.

She left the Texaco and followed the signs to the interstate.

She didn't have any problems until she pulled out of Mount Shasta's second entrance. She was the only car on the modified cloverleaf that took her onto I-5, but as she merged with the highway traffic, she felt the hair rise on the back of her neck.

She glanced in the rearview mirror.

A cop was behind her, with his lights on.

She hadn't done anything wrong that she knew of. But she had been preoccupied. And she had the bag of money on the seat beside her.

It looked suspicious.

She would have to play this coolly, hoping for the first time in her life that she had committed a moving violation, and that this was a routine stop.

The cop had pulled close to her bumper. She waved at him, followed the straightaway to a wide spot in the shoulder, and drove a few yards before pulling over. The cop pulled over behind her. She leaned across the book bag and opened the glove box, removing her registration and proof of insurance. Then she took her license from the fanny pack she had around her waist.

She rolled down her window. The air was cool and smelled of the mountains. The cop's police radio crackled and spit, voices sounding tinny and vague. She couldn't understand what they were saying. She wished she could.

The cop didn't come to her right away. She glanced

in the rearview mirror. He was sitting in the front seat of the squad car, writing something. Then he spoke into his radio.

Her stomach was doing cartwheels. She had never been pulled over before. She didn't know what normal procedure was.

Then his door opened, and he stepped out. Uniforms always unnerved her. He was thin, and had his hat pulled low almost to his eyes, which were hidden by sunglasses. He had a gun on his hip, and a small computer pad in his right hand. The fingers of his empty left hand rubbed together, nervously, it seemed, as if he were the one who had been pulled over.

When he reached her window, he removed the sunglasses, revealing a pair of dark brown eyes. "License and registration," he said.

She handed both to him, along with her insurance card. He studied them. A muscle beneath his right eye twitched. Color rose in his face. He took a deep breath, then leaned against the window.

"Ever hear of a rolling stop, ma'am?" he asked.

"Yes, sir," she said, her mouth dry. She licked her lips, wishing she knew how to hide her nervousness better.

"Well, we kinda let those go around here. Too many other violations to look into, you know?"

She frowned. He needed to get to the point. She couldn't stand it if he didn't.

"But, ma'am, you didn't roll through that stop on the access road. You barreled through. And I'm afraid I gotta ticket you."

She nodded, uncertain what to say.

"You seemed to be in a powerful hurry, Ms.—"

he glanced at her license "—Ms. Harding. Can I ask where you were going?"

"I have to get to San Francisco," she said. "A friend just called. He's sick."

"I'm sorry to hear that, ma'am," the officer said. "What's wrong?"

"What?" She hadn't expected this. Not in her wildest imagination. All she wanted to do was get out of town. She had never been pulled over in her life, and now this.

On the only day she didn't need it. That was how her life had been going lately.

"What's wrong with your friend, I mean."

She licked her lips again and then silently cursed herself for doing so. "He, um, didn't say. He just said he needed my help with his business."

"And what does your friend do?"

"Computers," she said because she didn't lie well.

The officer snapped his ticket book closed. He handed her license and registration back to her. Then he stepped away from the car.

"I'm sorry, Ms. Harding," he said. "But I need you to step out of the car."

Her heart was pounding so hard it felt as if it would go through her chest. "What did I say?" she asked.

"Ma'am, please, I don't want to ask you again." His voice rose. He was nervous. She had read articles about how dangerous cops get when they are nervous.

"Okay," she said. She glanced once at the book bag. He probably didn't want her to grab anything. She opened the door and slid out the side. As she stood beside the car, a truck went by on I-5, in a spray of gravel and exhaust. "What did I do?"

"Just put your hands on the car, ma'am, and spread your legs."

She did, feeling slightly foolish and more than a little terrified. The metal on her Rabbit was warm, and pocked with rust. If he searched her car and found all that money, he'd think she'd stolen it.

Maybe she had.

Maybe Steve had.

The cop patted her down with one hand, keeping the procedure as uninvasive as he could. "All right," he said. "You'll have to come with me."

"What did I do?" she asked again.

His face softened slightly. "I don't know, ma'am, but when I ran the check on your plates, I got a notice to bring you right in."

The bag. The money. She couldn't just leave it here.

"Can I drive myself?" she asked.

"No, ma'am. They suggest that I handcuff you. Someone will come out and bring your car into town."

So fast. They had caught her so fast. She had even used Steve's device and it had done no good.

She could run, but she had nowhere to go. No one to turn to. Except her mother. But what were the odds of getting to Chicago? And if the cops found her here, they'd certainly find her there.

She held out her hands for the cuffs. As he put them around her wrists, adjusting them for size, she said, "We have a problem, Officer. I have fifty thousand dollars in that book bag. It's not mine. It belongs to a friend. I was returning it. But I don't dare leave it here."

The cop raised a single eyebrow. He clearly didn't

believe her. "We'll put you in my car, and then I'll get your bag," he said.

She let him lead her to the squad car. He opened the door to the back seat and helped her inside. It smelled like old leather and sweat. The seat had been worn smooth. It reminded her of a taxicab, only the cabs she had been in had handles on the doors, and a sliding divider between her and the driver, not immobile plastic combined with mesh.

It had all happened so fast. She was a criminal, although she supposed she had been all along. Dialing the numbers for Steve, no matter how innocent it seemed, really wasn't.

The cop opened the front door and slid inside. He held her book bag up. It still bulged.

"I have your bag," he said. "You weren't kidding about the contents."

She could hear the unspoken question: Where'd a woman who drives a rusted-out twenty-some-year-old car get that kind of cash? But she also knew he wouldn't ask. He would leave it to the federal authorities. Too many people had gotten off because some lowly traffic cop had asked the wrong question without the proper warnings.

He started the car, waited for the traffic to clear, then drove across the median to the other side of the highway. Then, lights off, he drove her back to Mount Shasta.

But outside the city limits, he turned on a side road. She had been past the police station. It was in what Mount Shasta loosely termed its downtown.

Visions from all the bad movies she'd ever seen rose in her mind. She tried to force them back. She didn't need her overactive imagination at the moment.

"Where are you taking me?" she asked.

"The airstrip," he said. "The federal marshals should have a helicopter waiting for you."

"A helicopter?" she asked. Her hands were shaking. She didn't like this, didn't like the confinement. It made her think of her mother, which made her think of Leta Aider, which always, always upset her. "They're going to fly me somewhere?"

"New Mexico," he said, and, somehow, she wasn't surprised.

CHAPTER TWENTY-THREE

> Frae Witches, Warlocks, an' Wurricoes,
> An' Evil Spirits, an' a' Things
> That gang Bump i' the nicht,
> Guid Lord, deliver us!
>
> —INVOCATION

Loch Ness, March 15, 1986.

"I've seen her!"

Sam blinked awake. He'd heard something, but he wasn't quite sure if it was a dream or an actual event. He burrowed deep into the covers. Mrs. Comyn kept the inn cold at night. She followed the old-fashioned practice of having one of the help light a fire in each of the rooms at about dawn. Sam doubted she had many honeymooners as guests.

At least the bed was soft, and the quilts thick and warm.

"I've seen her!"

A door banged below, followed by running footsteps. Then the door to the room next to his opened.

"Travis?" Sammi Jo's voice sounded sleepy.

Sam moaned, remembering where he was, and realizing who the voice belonged to. He got out of bed, slid on a pair of pants and the flannel shirt he'd worn the night before. The hardwood floor was like ice beneath his bare feet. He ran a hand through his hair and pulled open his door.

"I've seen her!"

Travis was standing at the bottom of the curved stone stairs. The lights were on, reflecting his yellow rainslicker like a beacon. The floor behind him was wet—he had left a trail—and the air smelled damp.

"Stop yellin'," Sammi Jo hissed. "You'll wake everybody up." She was already halfway down the steps. She clutched her red robe closed with one hand and had the other pressed against the wall for balance. Her feet, beneath the robe, were long and narrow and bare.

"Too late," Sam said. "I think he's woken up all of the Highlands."

"I don't care!" Travis said. "I saw her."

"Who?" Sam asked.

"The monster," Sammi Jo said softly. "There ain't no other her, not for him."

He wondered at the touch of bitterness in her voice. He followed Sammi Jo down the stairs, hating the cold and the wooziness he felt, as if this were still part of his dream.

"It's still dark," he said.

"There's a moon," Travis said.

Sam remembered it, but also remembered it had been high when they'd had their discussion. It should have set long ago. "What time is it?"

" 'Tis early yet." Mrs. Comyn. She wore a nightshirt, and her hair, which Sam hadn't realized until that moment was long, was hanging down her back in a single graying braid. "Tell us about it, lad."

Of all of them, she seemed the least disturbed. She probably had been awakened a dozen times by guests who had "seen" the monster.

"I was sitting out on the dock," Travis said, his voice rising, "and something splashed. And then when I looked, I saw a head and a hump, rising out of the water. Right in the moonlight. She turned her head and looked at me, then swam across the water, sure as you please. Oh, Dix, she was glorious."

Sammi Jo had reached the bottom of the steps. She stopped beside him, still holding her robe closed. Her brown hair was sleep tousled. She looked as confused as Sam felt.

"Did you get pictures?" she asked.

"I hope so." He held out the camera. "Have you got a darkroom, Mrs. Comyn?"

"We barely hae a water closet, lad. But yer welcome to it." Then she smiled. "But I do hae equipment for ye. Some photographer left it behind last year. He'd been hoping to see Nessie, don't ye know, and she proved her elusive self. He stayed until two hours ta his flight, and then remembered he had ta drive ta Edinburgh. I never seen a man move so fast in me life. He promised ta send fer the equipment though'n he never did."

"I bet you find a lot of strange things," Sammi Jo said, politely.

"Ah, lass, ye dinna know. Just last week—"

"Let's go to it," Travis said. The conversation stopped. Sammi Jo sent Travis an angry glare, but

Mrs. Comyn seemed fine. The rudeness didn't seem to affect her at all.

"First you're going to dry off," Sam said to Travis, rebuking him without really directly confronting him. "You're tracking water all over Mrs. Comyn's clean inn."

" 'Tis the excitement, sir," she said. "It dinna matter."

"It matters. He can't stay in the wet clothes forever." Sam took the remaining steps, and when he reached the ground floor, he carefully stepped over the wet prints that Travis had made. "Have you ever set up a darkroom before?"

"No," Travis said.

"I have," Sam said. "Have Mrs. Comyn find you a suitable spot. I'll hang up your coat."

He took the slicker off Travis's shoulders. Water had beaded on the vinyl surface. As he moved it, the drops showered all over his nightclothes. Sam shuddered but said nothing.

"How did you get so wet?" Sammi Jo asked.

"It was raining," Travis said. He clutched the camera to his chest.

"I thought you said there was a full moon."

Good girl, Sam thought. He made his way toward the door, lingering long enough to hear Travis's reply.

"There was," he said. "The clouds were racing across it. There were moon-breaks."

"Moon-breaks." Mrs. Comyn laughed. " 'Tis a new one."

"Yes," Sammi Jo said in that same oddly bitter tone. "It is."

"The darkroom?" Travis said, seemingly oblivious to it all.

"That photographer," Mrs. Comyn said, "he was usin' the downstairs water closet. It should be fine fer ye. . . ."

Sam continued past them through the public room to the pegs for the coats. He hung the slicker on it, then peered out the bubbled glass windows.

The darkness was complete. There was no moon. His mother's voice came to him, speaking softly, hands on his shoulders as they stood on the porch of their home in Indiana.

It's always darkest before dawn, Sam.

Of course it was. The moon was down and the sun had yet to come up. But if the moon was down, it would have been down for some time. And Travis had only just awakened them.

Sam slid his feet in Angus's boots, then grabbed another coat from the wall. He didn't like the suspicions he felt, but he found comfort in knowing that Sammi Jo—who claimed to love Travis—felt them too.

The boots were too big, and their bottoms were flattened by years of use. The coat was too small and caught beneath his armpits. He opened the door and felt a blast of night cold hit him. There always seemed to be a wind over Loch Ness. He stepped onto the porch.

The sky was black with clouds. He saw no moon, although he remembered one from earlier. It had been high overhead. He needed to know the time. He needed to know if the moon had set.

He took a few steps forward. The loch looked like an oil stain on the earth. Its surface seemed flat, the hills beyond more black stains against the darkness.

The silence was eerie, and almost as compelling as Travis's story.

Perhaps he had seen something. Sam had heard that splash earlier. But seeing something and wanting to see something were two different things. Pretending to see something was another matter entirely.

He felt a shiver run down his back that had nothing to do with cold. How better for Travis to force his father's compliance with the project than to enact the plan they had had in the first place. Come to Loch Ness, see the monster, and get Daddy's backing for the very expensive search for the monster itself. In the process, solidify the relationship between father and son, and maybe win the hand of the fair Sammi Jo.

Sam frowned. He didn't know how much of his distaste for Travis was because of the young man's interest in Sammi Jo and how much was a reflected feeling from Harding himself.

And how much of it came from Sam.

He certainly found Travis exasperating, but he had no idea what Harding was like, although he had hints that the man was difficult at best.

Sam sighed, turned around, and came back inside. He removed the boots and the coat. The inside of the inn was nearly as cold as the outside. It only lacked the wind. He was now thoroughly chilled. Despite Loch Ness's gothic beauty, he didn't understand why anyone lived there.

He walked back across the public room to the hallway. Mrs. Comyn had turned on lights. She and Sammi Jo were huddled outside the downstairs water closet, with Travis inside blocking the only window.

"It has to be really dark," Sam said. He had set

up countless darkrooms in his early physics days. He'd had a professor who had used photography to teach the students about light.

"What took so long, Dad?" Travis asked, his tone neutral, his back to Sam.

He decided to tell the truth. "I looked outside, hoping I might get a glimpse myself."

"Ah, Nessie don't stay for longer'n a few minutes," Mrs. Comyn said. "I've said ta me da, I have, that I think the ole girl has a brain. She's been teasing tourists and Nessie watchers for generations now."

"That's one smart reptile," Sammi Jo said, smiling.

"Aye," Mrs. Comyn said. "I dinna believe all them reports about little brains. 'Tis the same as people who believe all animals are dumb. They should be at my back door near suppertime. Cats, dogs, all manner of creatures show up, and they dinna even hae the benefit a watches!"

"You going to help with the darkroom, Dad?" Travis asked. He had stepped down and was standing near the ancient claw-footed tub, arms crossed.

"Yeah," Sam said. "I wonder, though, if we shouldn't have some professionals verify this film. Maybe even develop it."

"And risk losing it or them lousing it up?" Travis asked.

"We have more of a chance of screwing up," Sammi Jo said.

"Dad says he's done this before."

"I have." Sam wanted to do it here anyway. He wanted to watch Travis. He wanted to make certain the film wasn't tampered with.

"Great," Travis said. He grinned, the smile making him seem younger. "You know if these photos come out, we'll be famous."

"Or you will," Sammi Jo said.

"What do you think of that, Dad?" Travis asked.

"I think we'd better not jump to conclusions until we've seen the film," Sam said.

"You don't believe I saw her, do you?"

Sam looked at Travis, saw the mixture of defiance and eagerness on the young man's face, and decided to ignore the hostility and go for compromise. "After you left me earlier this evening," he said slowly, "I heard a series of splashes in the loch. Big ones. But by the time I looked, all I saw was an empty surface and ripples leading away from a big disturbance. I thought it was fish, jumping to catch bugs."

"But you weren't sure," Sammi Jo said softly.

"But I wasn't sure," Sam said.

Mrs. Comyn laughed. "Even the hardened skeptic admits the loch has secrets." She clapped Sam on the back. "Ye need ta talk ta me da. He says he dinna believe in something he canna see."

Sam smiled wistfully. "I believe in many things I cannot see."

"He's a quantum physicist," Travis said. "They specialize in invisible things."

"But a lota people seen the monster," Sammi Jo said.

"Aye," Mrs. Comyn said. "Maybe even the laddie here. I'll go put on some tea, 'n' start an early breakfast. If ye need anathing, ye let me know."

"Where's the equipment?" Travis asked.

Mrs. Comyn shook her head good-naturedly. She didn't seem to notice Travis's rudeness at all. "I'd ferget me head if it wasn't tacked on. Come, lad. I'll show ye."

She led him through the narrow hall to the side of the water closet. He had to duck to go through. Sam watched him leave, then went to the window. Travis had used a piece of cloth. When the sun came up, light would stream through the tiny holes in the fabric.

"We'll need paper here, not cloth," Sam said.

"There's some on the sink," Sammi Jo said.

Sam grabbed a sheet, careful not to disturb the nails that were beside it. He ripped the cloth off the window, then put the paper over the glass, holding it with one hand.

"You really think he saw something?" Sammi Jo asked.

"Does it matter?" Sam asked. He grabbed the nails. "Travis does."

"Yeah, I suppose he does," she said, but she didn't sound convinced.

Sam turned to see the expression on her face, but by the time he did, she was gone.

CHAPTER TWENTY-FOUR

I drew a hard distinction between what I called the legal (past regarding) and the creative (future regarding) minds. I insisted that we overrated the darkness of the future, that by adequate analysis of contemporary processes its conditions could be brought within the range of our knowledge and its form controlled, and that mankind was at the dawn of a great changeover from life regarded as a system of consequences to life regarded as a system of constructive effort. I did not say the future could be foretold. We should be less and less bounded by the engagements of the past and more and more ruled by a realization of the creative effects of our acts.

—H. G. WELLS, *EXPERIMENT IN AUTOBIOGRAPHY*

Stallion's Gate, New Mexico, Now.

Al chomped on his cigar and pulled his bright red jacket closed. He had changed so that he would have a pocket for his cigars, but he hadn't given thought to the weather. The dry New Mexico heat was a bit much for his wardrobe. He had to cross from the main building housing the project to one of the smaller buildings near the gate. Visitors without security clearance never got past that area.

Of course he hadn't ordered a car. Of course he had insisted on walking to clear his mind.

He hadn't gone this long without contact with Sam since the Project had begun. Al finally realized how all the others felt—Gooshie, Tina, and Dr. Beeks. The feeling had a tinge of panic to it, as if Sam were in a serious accident, or a crisis.

Or as if he had vanished off the face of the earth.

The desperation made Al want to tear Ziggy apart, brilliant bit by brilliant bit, snotty chip by snotty chip, to see if somewhere in her massive memory she held the secret to Sam's whereabouts. But not even Ziggy, for all her confidence and pretensions, was infallible.

If only she were.

If she were, Project Quantum Leap would be a different kind of animal.

The base looked barren this morning. No jeeps, no cars, no workers crossing the brown expanse that everyone loosely called a lawn. The paved roads still had cracks from last summer's unrelenting heat, cracks made worse by the winter's abnormal chill. Al stepped gingerly over them, protecting his shiny red shoes—the ones that Tina called the Ruby Slippers—as best he could. Still they were getting covered with dust.

The building they had the girl housed in had once been used for storage. Al remembered it vividly. When he and Sam had started the Project, they had stored much of the equipment in that building, including many of Ziggy's component parts. It had since been remodeled into a bunkhouse for some of the older guards, the ones who didn't want to make the nightly two-hour drive to the nearest major town.

When Al reached the door, he took a deep breath, slicked his hair back with one hand, and brushed the dust off his clothes. Then he went inside.

The air in the building was artificially cool, just the way he liked it. Humid heat reminded him too much of 'Nam, but he found dry heat just plain unbearable. Two security guards stood near double doors, and a federal marshal sat behind a desk, hastily added to the hallway, filling out paperwork.

"Need you to sign off on this, Admiral," the marshal said, sliding a paper forward.

"What is it?" Al asked, glancing at the closed door.

"Formality, saying you brought the girl in for questioning, but that you don't plan to charge her with anything." The marshal frowned at him. "You don't, do you?"

"No," Al said. He grabbed a pen and scanned the document.

"Despite the money?"

"Money?" Al looked up.

"She had a book bag with fifty thousand dollars cash in it."

Al frowned. He had no idea where she got that, but if he was successful, it wouldn't matter. Even if he wasn't, it wasn't his concern.

Yet.

"I'm not going to do anything about the money," he said. "It's not against the law to carry a lot of cash, is it?"

"Um, no, sir," the marshal said. "But it is highly suspicious. Especially in this plastic age."

Al shrugged. ''If you don't qualify for plastic, how else can you survive?''

He scrawled his name, shoved the paper back to the marshal, and went inside the room.

The room could more accurately be called a space. It had high ceilings, no windows, and fluorescent lighting. The walls and floor were made of concrete. The space was empty except for the girl.

The girl sat in a chair in the center, her hands cuffed before her.

''Hey!'' Al said to the guards outside. ''I didn't call for any cuffs. Get those off her.''

They scurried in and, raising her arm, unlocked the cuffs. Samantha Josephine Fuller didn't watch them. She watched Al, her face bland and calm as if nothing were happening to her.

He'd seen that face before. On one of Sam's Leaps. The face of Abagail Fuller. She had been about the same age, too, when charged with the murder of Leta Aider. That unnerving calm seemed to run through the family, that ability to make even the most difficult situation seem as if it were a routine day at the office.

He knew, though, from that experience, that Sammi Jo must be torn up inside.

He waited until the guards were done. Then he closed the door. The sound made a booming echo in the vastness of the room. She watched him during the whole process, rubbing her right wrist with her left hand.

He decided to make this as friendly as he could. The handcuffs hadn't helped. He would have a lot to overcome. He stuck out his hand. ''Admiral Al Calavicci,'' he said.

''Admiral?'' Her voice was calm, soft, with a slight

Southern accent. "That's quite a rank. I'm afraid I don't have a rank. Or a serial number. Or," she added, smiling a bit, "a uniform quite like yours."

"This isn't an interrogation, Ms. Fuller," Al said.

She shook her head. "I've done a lot of reading, Admiral. I know that a lot of people get 'interviewed' without benefit of counsel, and then charged later. Sometimes those 'interviews' aren't thrown out by the courts."

Al bit back a curse. He didn't have time to play games, and he had a hunch that with her IQ Sammi Jo Fuller would be better at them than he was.

"Look," he said, "we both know that you illegally broke into our computer system. What you don't know is that Ziggy has a mind of her own. She *let* you hack your way into the system. If she hadn't wanted to talk to you, she would have cut you off."

"A computer would have cut me off," Sammi Jo said with disbelief.

"A parallel hybrid computer," Al said. "An artificial intelligence who would argue with you over the 'artificial' part."

Sammi Jo stuck out her chin. Defiantly, it seemed to him. "Why would she want to talk to me?"

Al took a deep breath. After his disastrous experience breaking the rules with Harding, he wasn't sure he even wanted to try to do so with this young woman, the one Ziggy had placed at the eye of the time storm. But he would if he had to.

"Because," Al said, "you were in Loch Ness with Dr. Donald Harding."

"He was my father-in-law," she said.

"Not at the time."

Something flashed across her face, almost too fast

to read. Then it disappeared and her features were smooth again. She was frightened. All of this terrified her.

It would probably terrify him too. Had terrified him when he'd been here in his younger days, as Bingo.

"Listen, sweetheart," Al said, "we're working on some important research and you actually hold key information."

"About my father-in-law."

"Yes," Al said. He fished in his pockets for some matches. "Mind if I smoke?"

"There's no ventilation in here," she said.

He glanced around. She was right. "I guess that's a no, huh?" he said.

She was still staring at him, her eyes narrowing. "You don't look like an admiral." She glanced pointedly at his shoes.

"You want me to get into my dress whites? The research facility isn't enough for you?"

She shook her head. "This is all just strange, you know. You want me to give you information about my father-in-law, but I haven't seen him since Loch Ness. I hook up with your computer, which has, from my understanding, something to do with time travel—"

"Ziggy told you that?" Al asked, shocked.

"Not exactly." She licked her lips. The gesture made her look younger than she was. "But you said we shouldn't be concerned with the details."

"Geez, kid," Al muttered. "I forgot about your photographic memory."

That surprised/frightened look flickered across her face again. Al would have loved to play poker against her. If, of course, she had been worth a lot of money.

And wasn't someone he knew.

Or related to someone he really cared about.

"What about time travel?" he asked.

"Well, I think it's odd, Admiral. You're doing time travel research, and my father-in-law has been investigating the physics of time travel ever since Loch Ness. In fact, his think tank specializes in it. I keep getting the feeling that you spent all those government dollars to bring me here because you're afraid I'm involved in some sort of corporate espionage for him."

Al put his cigar back in his mouth. It felt as if the bottom had dropped out of his stomach. He hadn't considered that at all.

And he hadn't known what Harding had done, in this life, with the information he got on the Leap. He had created his own think tank, his own way of coming to Sam's conclusions. A way that would use private dollars, corporate dollars.

Al had to remain calm. Harding wasn't the issue at the moment.

Sammi Jo was.

"Are you involved in corporate espionage?" Al asked.

"Honestly," she said, "no."

"Well then, that's settled." Or at least part of it was. When he got out of here, though, he'd go wring Harding's fat neck. The man had no plans to help Sam. From the moment Harding had seen Ziggy, he had clearly wanted all the glory for himself. And since the research was classified, he was soaking up as much of it as he could. Then, when he and Sam switched places, he'd go back and do what he could.

He was counting on remembering. And he must have, at least enough to start the think tank.

Obviously, it hadn't been quite enough. Al had no recollection or knowledge of anyone in the private sector doing legitimate work on time travel.

Al pulled out his handkerchief—red satin—and wiped his brow with it. The room needed ventilation—badly. "Since you're being honest with me, Ms. Fuller, I'll be honest with you. We're not interested in Dr. Harding's work now. We're interested in Donald Harding himself, specifically your recollections of him in Loch Ness in 1986."

"Why?"

Why? How could he answer why? "Why would take me three days to explain," Al said, "and I don't have that kind of time. What I need to know from you is did Donald Harding strike you as any different while you were in Loch Ness?"

"Different from what?" she asked.

"Different from how he was before."

She frowned at him, then sighed and pushed her hair back from her forehead. Her wrist was chafed from the handcuffs. Al would wring more than Harding's neck when he finished talking to Sammi Jo. He would have a word or two with those marshals as well.

"Look," she said. "Donald Harding is one of the cruelest men I've ever met. He didn't hit people or anything like that. He used words. And I remember that he was particularly cruel in Loch Ness."

Al wished there was a second chair in the room. He wanted to sink into it, maybe hide his face, take a moment to think. Sam wouldn't be cruel, not even unintentionally. Would he?

Maybe Harding was cruel to her before Sam arrived. Maybe that's what she remembered.

"Harding went out on Loch Ness by himself, didn't he? On the morning of March 14?"

She shook her head slightly. "You have an interesting command of the facts, Admiral," she said. "For something that was supposedly just three people's vacation. Do you keep detailed files like this on all Americans or is my family just lucky?"

"Your family is amazingly lucky," Al said with more sarcasm than he intended. "When he came back from that trip, did he act any different?"

"No," she said. "In fact, it was after that he and Travis had their big split."

Al crossed his arms. After? If Sam had arrived, he had done so on that loch. He had in the first Leap, the one Al had visited, and Al had no reason to believe that the subsequent change in the time line had changed that. But maybe Sam had changed something at Loch Ness, then Leaped elsewhere immediately. That had happened a lot, more than Al wanted to contemplate.

But Sammi Jo was his only hope. He would ask her a few more questions before giving up completely.

"What did they split over?" he asked.

"The photographs." She answered without hesitation.

"Photographs?" Al asked.

"Of the monster," she said. "Travis claimed he saw the Loch Ness monster during the night. He took a roll of photographs, and we developed them. They were dark, but there was clearly a reptile in them, a big, three-humped lizardlike creature with a skinny head, like the one in the Kenneth Wilson photo."

Al knew which one she meant. The most famous photo of the monster, taken in 1934, of a long, skinny neck with an angular snakelike head, rising out of the water. "The London surgeon?" he asked. "The guy who recanted on his deathbed?"

"His widow denies that," she said archly.

"So what was the fight over Travis's photos?"

She looked away, then ran a hand through her hair again, obviously a nervous gesture. "Dr. Harding had cause, you know? Travis went out in the middle of the night. He never did that—not before or since. Travis really likes his sleep. And he didn't wake me, which in those days he always did before he went somewhere. Then there was the problem of the moon."

"The moon," Al said. He felt light-headed. He really wanted to light his cigar.

"The moon." She looked up at him. She had a way of saying strange things as if everyone accepted them as fact, the way Abagail did. The way, come to think of it, Abagail's mother, Laura, did. "Travis claimed it was full—and it was. But it had been high in the sky and full just after dark, and by the time he said he saw the monster, the moon should have set. And then there was the matter of the rain."

"The rain," Al said.

"The rain." It felt like they were in a burlesque routine, only she didn't seem to notice. "Travis came in all wet, dripping water all over the floor, and he said it had been raining—"

"But he could see the moon."

"That's what bothered his father. Travis said the clouds were moving fast over the moon, but when Dr.

Harding checked it out, the sky was black and it didn't look like it had rained at all. Then when we developed the photos, the perspective was off. Dr. Harding mentioned that. He said that if you know how to use a camera, you can make a six-inch statue of a dinosaur look like the real thing. That's what old movie special effects were based on, you know.''

''I know,'' Al said dryly.

''And Travis blew up, saying that if his father didn't believe him after helping him develop the photographs, then his father would never believe him.'' She shook her head. ''And then it got real ugly. Calling each other names, screaming at the tops of their voices. We left before noon, and I never saw Dr. Harding again.''

''Dr. Harding called his son names?''

She winced. ''Not really. He implied that Travis wasn't telling the truth. It was pretty mild for Dr. Harding. Travis did all the name-calling. He seemed pretty satisfied with himself on that. He said for the first time that he'd finally gotten a word in edgewise.''

''And what happened to Dr. Harding?''

She shrugged.

''Didn't he try to contact Travis?''

''Sure,'' she said. ''And then, when that failed, he tried to go through me. But that didn't work either.''

''So you believed Travis.''

''I didn't say that,'' she said.

Al looked at her.

''I didn't exactly disbelieve him.'' She licked her lips. ''At the time, anyway. Later, I don't know.''

''He faked things later.''

''Yes. No. Some things. The hotline is for money, you know.'' She peered at him through her hair. She made it seem as if she were making an earth-shattering revelation.

"I figured as much," Al said.

"So do most people," she said, "but I didn't. There are such things in the world, Admiral, as psychics and ghosts, whether people want to believe it or not. You just can't tie them to phone lines."

"If only you could," Al said. He was getting nowhere with her. And from her description, Sam hadn't stayed in Harding. That made things a lot worse. Then he frowned, one of her words suddenly becoming clear to him.

Ghost. Sometimes, children who saw Al in his holographic state called him a ghost.

"You ever see a ghost?" Al asked.

She crossed her arms and leaned back in the chair as if to get away from him. "What?"

"In Loch Ness, maybe?"

"Why don't you just ask if I've seen the monster?"

"Did you?"

"No," she said.

"And no ghosts," Al said.

"No," she said.

Al raised his eyebrows. "Tender topic."

"Just because people thought my gramma was touched doesn't mean I am," she said.

She must have heard that accusation a lot. Being with Travis probably made it worse.

"I wasn't implying that," Al said. "I was only wondering—"

"You can't get on my good side by pretending you believe in ghosts, goblins, and things that go bump in the night. That's where Dr. Harding made his mistake."

Al froze. "His mistake?"

"He thought he could use my gramma's psychosis to—I don't know—get buddy-buddy with me, maybe, or to use it as proof that I was as crazy as she was, and therefore not good enough for his son."

Al took the cigar out of his mouth. He couldn't seem too eager on this. He might be reading too much into it. "Your grandmother's psychosis?"

"You claim to know about my family," she said. "If you've read my gramma's records, you know she believed in a walk-in named Sam."

"Yes," Al said. His heart was beating faster than before. "She claimed she saw a man named Sam who looked different from the men he was supposed to be."

"Well, a few hours after I told Dr. Harding about that, he claimed he was that Sam. It was one of the meanest things anyone ever said to me—"

"Mean?" Al frowned at the word. "Mean?"

"He was mocking me. He knew how important it all was, and he was mocking me."

"Maybe he wasn't," Al said. Al's heart was pounding. He hadn't felt this much hope since the Leap began. "I gotta get to Ziggy."

"Why?" Sammi Jo asked.

"I don't have time to answer," Al said. "At least not right now." And he hoped later he wouldn't have to.

He shoved his cigar in his mouth and pounded on the door, asking to be released. Then he nodded to Sammi Jo. "Thanks for your help. You don't know what this means to me. To all of us."

The door opened, and Al startled the guards by running past them. Behind him, he could hear Sammi

Jo shouting after him, demanding to know who Sam was, and why he was important.

If she only knew, Al thought, as he ran across the compound. If she only knew.

CHAPTER TWENTY-FIVE

The gift of second sight, or prophecy by visions is, of course, not peculiar to Scotland; but it seems to have flourished more—and still does flourish more—in the mystic Celtic atmosphere of Scotland than almost anywhere else on earth.

—RONALD MACDONALD DOUGLAS,
SCOTTISH LORE AND FOLKLORE

Loch Ness, March 15, 1986.

Dixie stood outside the makeshift darkroom. The old-fashioned electric lights, designed to resemble gaslights—or perhaps simply there to replace them—gave the hallway a dark orangish look. She had slipped on her Shetland sweater and her jeans, but her feet in their cheap tennis shoes were still cold. There wasn't enough space for her in the tiny room, not for her, anyway, and Dr. Harding and Travis. Travis had made it clear that he wanted his father in there.

To prove, of course, that the pictures were not falsified. Maybe even to convince the man that his son had been right all along.

She felt an odd nervousness, not liking the thoughts

that had been crossing her mind since Travis woke them all with his yelling. He had been so determined to convince his father. He had said that his father needed hard evidence.

And now, hard evidence might be within their grasp.

But the hard evidence was so convenient. The one thing she knew from all her experience with the odd phenomena of the world was that when you wanted something magical to happen, it never did. No matter how hard you believed. No matter how much you wished.

It never happened.

And yet, Travis, alone, had seen the monster.

She ran a hand through her fine hair. She hadn't washed it since the previous morning, and the strands fell limply around her face. Travis never did anything alone. He always brought her along. He always said he needed witnesses, and she had always smiled.

Suddenly she wasn't a witness anymore.

And the tiny toy model of the monster they had bought at the museum shop in Drumnadrochit, her first birthday gift from Travis, was missing from the nightstand. She had noticed when she turned on the light that the model wasn't in the water they had poured in the washbowl, the place she had put it in a moment of whimsy.

She put a fist against her stomach, not liking these thoughts. She was in love with Travis. She shouldn't suspect him so. He was a good man. She had known that from the beginning.

He was the only one who had met her family, indeed who had heard the history of her family, and not let it affect him. He had stood beside her. He had believed in her.

Sometimes I think he's as interested in them as he is in me.

She pushed the fist harder into her stomach. She hated Dr. Harding for pulling that sentence out of her. She hated him for trying to trap her with that story, and then for making her warm to him by the end of the conversation.

Travis was right; his father was a great manipulator, cruel and selfish as all manipulators were. Who cared if Travis had made up the sighting in order to get his father's help? A father should help his child without question.

A father should always believe in his child.

A father should always be there for his child.

"Na, lassie, ye canna wait here all night." Mrs. Comyn was standing behind her. Dixie forced herself to smile as she turned.

"I'll be all right," she said.

"Na without a bit a nourishment." Mrs. Comyn handed her a delicate teacup filled to the brim, and a scone covered with clotted cream.

Dixie hated clotted cream, but she nodded her thanks. She took a sip from the tea and found that it warmed her.

"I must go 'n' fix me da's breakfast. He's trawlin' this morning, he is, 'n' dinna wan the 'nonsense with the monster' as he calls it, getting in his way." Then Mrs. Comyn smiled. She looked like a girl. " 'Tis exciting, though, the idea that your young man may hae snaps a the creature."

"Yes, it is," Dixie said. She broke a piece off the end of the scone, the end without the cream, and ate it. Her stomach rumbled, and she hadn't even realized she was hungry. "I appreciate this," she said.

" 'Tis nothing, lass. I'll be back after me da sets out."

"Maybe by then, they'll have photos for you."

Mrs. Comyn laughed. She started down the hall, and then she paused. "Ye know, yer welcome ta join us, lass. I do a big breakfast fer me da when he's trawlin'."

"This'll be enough, thanks," Dixie said. She waited until Mrs. Comyn disappeared down the hall, then set the teacup down. She used her finger to scrape the cream off the scone. Then she slid down the wall, stretched out her legs, and had a small feast.

Her head was leaning against the makeshift darkroom's door. Yet she couldn't hear anything from inside. If they were talking, they weren't talking loudly, which was probably a good sign. She took another sip from the tea and closed her eyes. Maybe a small nap would help this unease growing in her belly.

Maybe.

Then she heard an odd sound, as if someone were opening a refrigerator door. No, that was wrong. It had the pneumatic whoosh of those electronic doors at an American supermarket.

She opened her eyes and saw a strange square blue light at the end of the hall. A man stood in the middle of it. He was short, with dark hair and intense eyes. He held a multicolored box in one hand, a cigar in the other.

When he saw her, he smiled. "It worked," he said. Then he shouted, "Ziggy! It worked!"

She pinched herself, literally, to see if she was dreaming. The pain in her arm convinced her she wasn't. She had never had a dream this vivid. The pinch felt real enough. The tea and half-eaten scone was beside her. The hall was still narrow and cold.

But the light was blue, and the man had his head tilted as he watched her watch him.

"You can see me, can't you, kiddo?" he asked, frowning at her.

She stood all the way up. She was as tall as he was. His red suit looked like it was made in the seventies, except for the material. He wore matching red shoes. They had dust on them.

"Sammi Jo," he said. "Can you see me?"

He knew her name. Her real name. Her gramma's insanity had finally found her. Her eyes filled with tears. Not now. Not yet.

"What do you want?" she asked, struggling to keep her voice level.

"I need to find Sam—ah, Dr. Harding. Do you—?"

"No!" she screamed the word without even realizing she was doing it until the force of it ripped through her throat. "No! Go away! No!"

The man put out his hands as if to calm her. "Now, Sammi Jo, listen," he said. "It's impor . . ."

He faded out. The blue light was momentarily gone. She was shaking.

". . . tant." He flickered back in. Then he glanced at his hands. "Did I fade?" he asked. "Did something just happen?"

She nodded.

"Ziggy!" He paused, and shook his cigar at her. "Wait here," he said. Then he walked through the blue light and disappeared.

She was breathing hard, and she couldn't move.

Mrs. Comyn was coming from down the hall. Dixie could hear the woman's bustling gait.

Then the darkroom door opened, and Dr. Harding slipped out, apparently without letting any light inside. Travis followed.

''What happened?'' Harding asked.

Dixie looked at him. Her lower lip trembled. His face was filled with compassion. She didn't want to see the compassion. ''I don't know how you did that,'' she said. ''But it was mean.''

''What did he do?'' Travis asked. His features held no compassion at all. In fact, he looked angry at the interruption.

Mrs. Comyn stopped a few feet away from them. ''Is ev'rathin' all right here?'' she asked.

''Fine,'' Dixie said, ''except Dr. Harding is one of the meanest people I ever did meet.''

''What did I do?'' He sounded genuinely perplexed.

''Is there equipment down there, Mrs. Comyn, or are you in on it too?''

''Equipment, lass?''

''To make a blue door. You know, lights.''

''What are you talking about?'' Travis snapped.

''The blue door. That strange little man. Asking for Sam.'' She faced Dr. Harding as she said it. ''You couldn't leave it alone, could you? You had to try one more time. You want to push me over that same edge my gramma fell over. Well, it won't work.''

''He asked for Sam?'' Harding said. He grabbed Dixie's shoulders. ''A blue light and a man who asked for Sam.''

She shook herself free. ''Stop pretending. I'll leave now. I don't want to be mixed up in your family anymore. It worked, Dr. Harding. I don't want to be near none of you."

"Don't leave, Dix," Travis said. "We're so close. You should see the photos—"

"I don't want to see the photos," she said. She had to get away from them, both of them. Travis's anger, and his father's games.

"Sammi Jo—" Dr. Harding said.

"My name is Dixie!" she snapped. "Dixie. Don't presume to call me Sammi Jo. My family calls me that. No one else."

Then she heard that odd *whoosh!* again. She turned. The blue light was blocking Mrs. Comyn.

"Oh, not again," Dixie said.

Dr. Harding turned in the wrong direction. Travis was still staring at her. Mrs. Comyn walked through the light just as the strange little man did too. His image shivered around her. Then Mrs. Comyn stood in front of him. She didn't seem to notice him at all.

"There," the man said. "That's better. Listen, Sammi Jo—"

"No!" she yelled and ran away, away from them all, up the stairs to her room, the room she shared with Travis. She would pack and leave them to their bickering and their squabbling—and their meanness. She'd write a letter to Mrs. Comyn, thanking her for her kindness, and that would be it. That would be all. She would then put this whole event behind her.

Strange little men and all.

"Sammi Jo!" The strange man had a voice like gravel. It mingled with the others.

"Dixie!" Travis yelled. "Come back here."

"Lass!"

But Dr. Harding wasn't yelling. He of the practical

jokes. She reached her room and stopped, breathing hard. The door was open, the bed, pushed against the slanted ceiling, was unmade, her robe thrown across it.

Maybe she wouldn't give him the satisfaction of leaving. Maybe she would—

"Sammi Jo, look, I know this is upsetting you, but I need to talk to Dr. Harding and I need your help."

The strange man was standing in the doorway. The blue light was gone, but he still held the multicolored remote in one hand, and the cigar in the other. He looked more like a carny at a circus than a ghost. The next time, she would tell Dr. Harding, he should have his fake ghost wear a bedsheet.

She went up to him and ran a hand through him. His image reflected on her skin, like a projection would. She glanced around, looking for cameras, for anything that would explain this.

The man moved away from her. This was an excellent image. "Listen, kiddo," he said. "We don't have a lot of time."

Dixie backed into the room. She needed to get away from this place, from everyone here.

"Sammi Jo . . ." Dr. Harding ran through the strange man and stopped in the center of the room. The man's image wavered for a moment, then reformed. The man shook his head and grinned.

"Sam!" the man said. "Sam!"

But Dr. Harding didn't turn around.

"You can stop this game now," she said. "Go back downstairs, be with Travis, and *leave me alone.*"

"Sam," the man said. "Sam, it's me. Al. Sam."

‘‘It’s not a game,’’ Dr. Harding said. ‘‘Please. It’s important that I talk to Al.’’

‘‘Then talk to him!’’ Dixie snapped. She got her suitcase from the wardrobe. It was lighter than she expected. She swung it onto the bed, narrowly missing Dr. Harding.

‘‘He can’t see me,’’ the man, Al, said. ‘‘Only you can, Sammi Jo.’’

She put her hands over her ears. ‘‘Play your games somewhere else,’’ she said.

‘‘It’s not a game,’’ Al and Dr. Harding said in unison.

She sighed and brought her hands down. ‘‘Oh, of course it’s a game. And Travis is just like you, tryin’ to trick you into believin’ in the monster. You’re tryin’ to see if I believe in ghosts. Well, maybe I would if he looked like a ghost. Instead, he looks like he belongs on an ‘Oprah’ episode for the fashion-impaired.’’

‘‘Hey!’’ Al said.

‘‘Al?’’ Dr. Harding whispered. ‘‘Are you here?’’

‘‘Of course I’m here,’’ Al said, but Dr. Harding didn’t seem to hear him. That didn’t phase Al. He turned to Dixie. ‘‘And I’ll have you know, kiddo, that this suit cost more than your entire vacation.’’

‘‘That’s a recommendation for clothing—’’ Dixie said, ‘‘cost. The more expensive it is, the better it looks. I can’t believe someone would believe that.’’

‘‘I’m taking fashion advice from a woman wearing the remains of a sheep?’’

‘‘It’s not the remains,’’ she snapped. ‘‘It’s sheared and spun. And people all over the world adore these sweaters.’’

‘‘Al,’’ Dr. Harding said, turning around like a blind

man. "Al, stop arguing about clothing, and talk to me. How come I can't see you?"

"Tell him—"

Dixie shook her head. She pushed past Dr. Harding and got clothes out of the wardrobe. "I'm not going to tell him anything. You tell him."

"I can't tell him," Al said.

"I can't see him," Dr. Harding said plaintively. He was a better actor than she would have expected.

"And I'm the pope," Dixie said, wishing she had a wittier comeback.

"He can't see me or hear me," Al repeated, "and I need to talk to him."

Dixie sighed and crossed her arms. She had to look at the projection because she couldn't see the camera. Still, she felt a bit silly talking to someone who wasn't there. "Even if I believed this for one small second," she said, "why would I be able to see you and he can't? Is he that bad a scientist?" She turned to Dr. Harding. "Are you?"

Dr. Harding sighed and clenched his fist. "Something went wrong with the experiment, Dixie."

"You're in the eye of a time storm, girl," Al said. "And somehow, I can only reach you."

Dixie shook her head. "This is good. This is really good. Play on my lack of education." She walked over to Al and ran her hand through him again. A slight tingle went up her arm, and the effect was eerie, but this time she had expected it.

"I'm not as dumb as you think," she said. "I know how some special effects work, and I read about them 3-D projectors they've been developing at MIT. In undergraduate physics there, they been teaching kids how to make holograms."

"How'd you know that?" Dr. Harding asked, stunned.

"I was on the ARPAnet for a while, okay?" she said. "I had a boyfriend from MIT 'til he met my family. That's why this is such a cruel joke. Now end it."

"It's not a joke," Al and Dr. Harding said in unison. Then Al stopped, but Dr. Harding went on, as if he hadn't even heard Al.

"If it is a joke," Dr. Harding said, "find the projection equipment. And when would I have set it up? And why?"

"You got here first," she said. "Maybe you did it to freak Travis and decided I was an easier target."

"Then find the equipment."

"We don't have time, Sam," Al said.

"There would have to be cameras, projectors," Dr. Harding said, his voice covering Al's protests.

Dixie shrugged, feeling the beginning of doubt form in her mind. "I wouldn't know what to look for."

"Then ask Al to do something unexpected. Something we couldn't have planned for."

She shook her head and sank on the bed. "Where's Travis?" she asked.

"Back in the darkroom."

"Alone?"

"Why?" Dr. Harding asked. "Is that a problem?"

"No more than your friend here," Dixie said. She sighed. "All right. I'll play along for a minute. You two can have your laugh, and I'll leave. It certainly won't be the worst thing that's happened to me." She ran a hand through her hair. "Dr. Harding, your pal 'Al' is standing by the door, wearing one of the ugliest red suits I ever seen in my life. In case you didn't know."

Dr. Harding turned. He looked at a spot beside the door. His acting was good. If she didn't know better, she would have thought he really couldn't see this Al at all.

"What's going on?" Dr. Harding asked the air. "Where have you been?"

"Trying to find you," Al said. He at least was looking at Dr. Harding. Dixie didn't know how they achieved that effect.

"He says he's been tryin' to find you." Dixie kept her voice calm.

"I've been here all along, Al." Dr. Harding said. Nice, convincing dialogue. She didn't believe it for a second.

"Can he understand you or do I have to translate that too?" she asked.

"I can hear him," Al said.

"Good." She grabbed more clothes out of the wardrobe. They could play their little game, but she was going to get packed.

"Tell him there's been a time storm," Al said. "Tell him we can't find him, but we latched onto you."

Dixie turned to Al. He looked so intense, so sincere. "Lucky for me," she said and rolled her eyes. Dr. Harding was watching her, waiting. "Your buddy Al claims there was a 'time storm' and he could find me, but not you."

"A time storm," Dr. Harding said to her because, she thought, he was pretending he couldn't see the projection. "Major changes? Lots of swirling?"

"Yeah," Al said.

Dixie nodded.

"I must have changed something important, Al," Dr. Harding said, turning his head toward the door.

"Oh, you did," Al said, "and this little girl is the center of it."

She hated that. She hated being patronized. She could put up with the joke, and the rudeness, and the dismissal. But she was tired of being treated like she was a child.

She tossed her clothes on the bed. "All right. It stops here. I am not a little girl. I haven't been for years, really, and I'm really sick of this. You boys can play this game without me."

"Have you been insulting her, Dad?" Travis was standing in the door, his body half overlapping Al's. Al moved away, an expression of distaste crossing his face.

"He's playing a dumb game," Dixie said. "You know how to look for fake holographic projections, right? Will you find that one?"

Travis frowned at her. "What one?"

"That one," she snapped. "The one you're standing on."

Travis looked around. Al had moved out of his way. He had lit his cigar and was puffing it, blowing rings of smoke in Travis's face. Dixie couldn't smell the cigar, and Travis didn't even try to brush the rings away.

"I don't see anything, Dix," Travis said.

He really looked like he didn't. She felt a chill. "You don't see that weird little man in red?"

"I resent that," Al said.

"Serves you right after that 'little girl' comment," Dixie said.

"What little girl comment?" Travis asked. "What's going on here?"

"Sammi Jo thinks she's seeing a ghost," Dr. Harding said. "Do you see one?"

Travis crossed his arms and glared at her. "Come on, Dix, there's not supposed to be ghosts in Loch Ness."

"It's some kinda projection," Dixie said. "Are you in on this with your father?"

"With my father?" Travis said, and she knew immediately that was absurd. The two couldn't even eat a meal together civilly. They certainly couldn't plan a practical joke together.

Dixie felt the color leave her face. "You mean you really don't see that little man?"

"What man?" Travis's voice was rising. She recognized that sound. Pretty soon he was going to explode.

"That guy in the corner, wearing neon red? You don't see him?"

"Dixie," Travis hissed. "Don't wreck this."

"Wreck what?" she asked.

"There can't be a monster *and* a ghost."

Dr. Harding was watching all of this, a raised eyebrow revealing his amusement. Al had moved closer to Travis. "Come on, kid," he said, "show 'em all what you're made of."

Travis didn't even seem to hear.

"Why not?" Dixie asked. "Why can't there be a monster and a ghost?"

"It's too incredible," Travis said. "No one would believe that."

"But they'd believe just a monster?"

Travis's gaze flickered to his father.

"Now's the time to confess, son," Al said. "Tell them you spent the night splashing about in the lake, setting up those fake photos."

"Of course," Travis said. "Lots of people have seen the monster."

"But you didn't, did you, Travis?" Dixie didn't know why that disappointed her so. Or maybe she did. She had wanted to believe in him, always. Because if she couldn't believe him about this, she might not be able to believe he loved her for herself, rather than her strange past.

"I saw it," he said, but the denial sounded false. "Come on, Dix. I'll show you the photos."

"I don't want to see any photos," she said, "and I don't want to translate for your damn ghost."

She whirled, feeling slightly dizzy, grabbed her clothes, and started shoving them in the suitcase.

"Dixie," Travis said.

"Sammi Jo, please," Dr. Harding said. "Continue. Please."

She looked up at him, then glanced at Travis. Then froze. Al was gone. Not even smoke rings remained.

She put a hand to her forehead—the dizzy feeling was still there—and sat on the edge of the bed. "He's gone," she said.

"What?" Dr. Harding actually sounded panicked. "Gone? He can't be."

"He is," she said. "Nice timing, turning the projection off when my back was turned."

"What projection?" Travis asked. "Will someone tell me what's going on?"

"Nothing," Dr. Harding said. His voice was shaking, and his eyes looked empty.

"You can stop pretending now," Dixie said. "I'm

impressed with your skill. You're better at it than your son. Physics is probably the way to go. Use science to screw people.''

She reached over and tried to shut her suitcase, but it was too full.

''What do I pretend about?'' Travis asked. He sounded hurt.

She sat on the case and zipped it closed. ''Everything, Travis,'' she said. ''I been tryin' to ignore it, but it don't work. I gave you credibility. But I'm done doing that now. You've never been interested in strange phenomena for its own sake. You always been interested in what you could get out of it. It's always about you, never about the occurrence. And I don't like that, any more than I like bein' tricked.''

''It wasn't a trick,'' Dr. Harding said.

She picked up the suitcase, wincing at its weight. ''Yes, it was,'' she said. ''We both know that. Nicely done, though, I must admit. You and Travis should hook up. You'd have a nice scam going.''

She grabbed her coat off the chair and headed toward the door. She stopped in front of Travis. ''I'm taking our car,'' she said. ''You can catch a ride with your father.''

And then she left.

CHAPTER TWENTY-SIX

It may seem a Paradox to others, but to me it appears undeniable, that the Scottish idiom . . . is more fit for pleading, than either the English idiom, or the French tongue; for certainly a pleader must use a brisk, smart and quick way of speaking . . .

—SIR GEORGE MACKENZIE,
PLEADINGS IN SOME REMARKABLE CASES BEFORE THE SUPREME COURTS OF SCOTLAND (1673)

Loch Ness, March 15, 1986.

Sam stood dumbfounded. Something had changed. Sammi Jo was leaving. Al was already gone, and Sam had no notion what had happened. Travis was staring at Sam as if Sammi Jo's entire blowup had been his fault.

The wardrobe doors stood open, and the light had started coming through the windows.

It was dawn.

"Are you going to let her go?" Sam asked.

Travis shrugged. "I didn't know she could be so rude."

"Maybe she felt pushed."

"Maybe." The voice belonged to Al. Sam turned. He hadn't heard the door open. But Al stood behind him just the same, handlink in his left hand, cigar in his right.

"Al!" Sam said.

Al brought his cigar to his lips in a motion for silence.

"What?" Travis asked.

"You really don't have time to talk, Sam," Al said. "Ziggy's ninety-nine percent sure you're here for Sammi Jo, and if she leaves now, she won't marry Travis, but she won't work at the lab, either."

"Work at the lab?" Sam asked.

"What?" Travis asked again.

"Um . . ." Sam looked at him, wondering what he had said out loud. "I mean, are you done in the darkroom?"

"No," Travis said.

"Finish up. I'll go after Sammi Jo."

"Dixie," Travis mumbled. But he headed down the stairs. Sam ran past him, through the narrow hallway, and out the door.

The loch was shrouded in fog. The light was gray and white at the same time, and the air was chill. Nearby trees dripped, and a bird's cry echoed in the solitude.

"Over here, Sam!" Al stood at the side of the inn, just past the rock garden. Sam ran toward him.

"I can't tell you how good it is to see you," Sam said.

"Likewise, buddy," Al said. "But you gotta find her."

Sam nodded. He hurried toward the back of the inn. He had gone out the wrong door. As he reached the outbuildings, he heard the sound of an engine straining to start.

"Do you know what happened?" he asked as he ran.

"We got an idea," Al said. "Ziggy thinks Harding was supposed to convince Sammi Jo to go to college and study physics, although I don't think Harding could convince Elizabeth Taylor to buy diamonds."

"Who?" Sam asked.

"Never mind," Al said. "I just don't think Harding could inspire anyone."

"If the feelings I got about him were true," Sam said, "I agree."

"So that leaves it up to you, Sam."

"What?" Sam asked.

"She can't leave here without wanting to study physics. She was at the lab until you Leaped here, and Ziggy says she might be the one to bring you home."

"My own daughter?"

"Your kid. Makes sense, doesn't it?" Al asked.

"And if I don't convince her?"

"Well, first she married Travis, and that screwed things up so bad that I couldn't find you. And now she's not going to marry that nozzle, but she isn't going to college either, unless you do something."

The car wheezed and choked. The fog carried the sound—and the smell of petrol—through the air.

Sam stopped running. He was breathing a bit too hard. "I can't, Al. I can't convince her of anything. She hates me."

"You, Sam?"

"Me, Harding, whomever. She didn't trust him, and I made things worse."

"You gotta try, Sam."

Sam took a deep breath. He walked forward, and through the fog a battered lime green Peugeot appeared. It had British plates on the back. Sammi Jo's suitcase was in the front seat. She was beside the suitcase, on what seemed like the wrong side to Sam, even though the steering wheel was in front of her. As the car chugged then seemed to die, she brought her forehead down until it touched the steering wheel.

Sam glanced at Al. Al waved his arm in that go-on signal he did so well. Sam knocked on the window.

Sammi Jo snapped her head up. "What do you want?"

Her voice was muffled through the glass.

Sam bit his lips. He had to try. She didn't trust him, and he couldn't seem to gain that trust, not in a heartbeat.

But if he couldn't gain trust, maybe he could play on her distrust.

"I want to apologize," he said.

"Sure." She sounded sarcastic, but she rolled down the window anyway. "Apologize for what?"

"Trying to manipulate you."

"Sam!" Al said.

"I knew it," she said, but she didn't look vindicated. She looked sad. "Well, it worked. I'm gettin' as far away from you and Travis as I can."

"That wasn't it," Sam said. "I wanted to get you to use your mind."

"My mind." She looked at him sideways. "How?"

"I told you about physics. I wanted you to see its possibilities. I thought maybe you might try to debunk what I did, to get to the bottom of 'Al.' Instead, you got mad and left."

"Just like a woman," she said. She turned the key in the ignition, and the car screeched. She brought her hand back as if she had been burned. "Guess it was already running."

"So I came out to apologize." Sam's heart was pounding. He was screwing this up. One of his most important Leaps and he had destroyed it by breaking all the rules.

"I'm not gonna go back in," she said.

"I'm not asking you to."

"And I'm not gonna make up with Travis."

"That's your choice," Sam said.

"Then what do you want?"

"To see if I could repair the damage I did."

She sighed and leaned her head back. "What's so important about me and physics?"

"Nothing," Sam said, "except that I think you might have a talent for it."

"Me, the girl who didn't finish math in high school."

"Yes," Sam said. "I think that was a waste of talent and energy. You figured out the hologram, and you showed some innate scientific talent earlier. You figured out how Travis faked his photographs without even looking at them."

"It wasn't hard when I saw the plastic monster was gone from our room," she said.

"The thing is that you have a gift, Sammi Jo. Most people aren't given the mind you have, and you let petty people like that math teacher of yours, and—" Sam took a deep breath "—and even people like me stop you from developing that mind to its full potential.''

''Just 'coz I believed Travis when he proposed this trip, don't mean I wasn't usin' my mind,'' she said.

''No,'' Sam said. ''That's not what I mean. A good scientist has to believe in the impossible. Otherwise we don't get anywhere. Don't you see, Sammi Jo? Science isn't about proving what is. Science is about discovering what can be.''

She turned to him. ''I thought scientists quantified the known universe,'' she said.

''Some of them do. Then others work on a grander scheme. Astronomers study the stars—but they don't see every star. They have to work on speculation. We can observe Saturn's rings, but we don't know what caused them. We only have theories. It works that way through all branches of science. My branch just has a bit more mysticism than others.''

''Mysticism.'' Her tone was sarcastic, but her eyes sparkled. He remembered that sparkle from her childhood, the brief moments he'd had with her, talking about the future.

''Quantum physics deals with things we can't see. Quarks, string theories, grand unification theories. They have so many possibilities, so many applications. Wouldn't you like to know if time travel is possible? What about ghosts? Maybe they are some kind of projection, like the hologram you saw—''

''Sam,'' Al cautioned, but Sam ignored him. He liked the slightly gap-mouthed expression growing on his daughter's face.

''—or maybe they're something else. Energy remnants. We don't know what the spark of life is yet, Sammi Jo. We don't know what the essence of us is.

We do know that when we die, the body loses a tiny, tiny percentage of weight, enough, some say, to carry a soul. What if souls can travel outside of their bodies? What if—''

''Astral projection?'' she asked.

''Whatever you want to call it,'' he said. ''What if your grandmother was right? What if there are walk-ins—''

Sammi Jo shook her head.

''—and what if there is a scientific explanation for them?''

She raised an eyebrow. ''What if prehistoric creatures do live at the bottom of Loch Ness?''

''That's right,'' Sam said. ''Think of the possibilities.''

His words echoed in the fog-drenched morning. The bird called again, and something splashed on the loch. Sammi Jo sighed and leaned her head back on the ripped car seat.

''You tried to have this discussion with Travis, didn't you?''she asked.

''Yes,'' Sam said.

''He's too angry at you to listen.'' She raised her head and looked at him directly. ''And you're not the most tactful man in the world.''

''I know,'' Sam said.

Al came a step closer. His presence calmed Sam. Sam hadn't realized exactly how much he had missed Al until now.

''He's just like you, you know,'' she said. ''He can't just believe in something. He needs proof. That's all he wants. Proof something magical exists.''

''Proof sometimes takes the magic away,'' Sam said.

‘‘And sometimes it adds the magic.’’ She ran a hand through her hair and shook her head. ‘‘I’m sorry I accused you.’’

‘‘I’m sorry I was such an idiot,’’ Sam said. ‘‘Are you going to come back in?’’

She nodded. ‘‘We gotta get them photographs away from Travis before he embarrasses himself.’’

‘‘Go on,’’ Sam said. ‘‘It would probably be better if it came from you rather than me. I’ll get your stuff out of the car.’’

She smiled, then let herself out. She still gave him a wide berth, but she didn’t seem as hostile as she had before.

Sam reached inside the car and turned the key in the ignition. The car stopped shaking. ‘‘What a bolt-bucket,’’ he said.

‘‘Cheap rental,’’ Al said. He was staring at the handlink.

‘‘How’d that go?’’ Sam asked.

‘‘You did it, Sam. At least I think so. Ziggy reports the time storm gone. Sammi Jo goes on to college—and not just any college. First she goes to CalTech, then she does her graduate work at MIT, and her post-doc at Harvard. That’s some kid you have.’’

Sam smiled.

‘‘She doesn’t marry the nozzle, but she does keep dating him for another year. They have an amicable breakup and are still friends.’’ The handlink squealed and Al hit it. ‘‘The kid gives up all this mystical stuff. He goes back to UCLA so he can be near Sammi Jo, and while he’s there, he discovers paleontology. He’s now in some South American dig.’’ Al smiled. ‘‘Well, he didn’t change completely. The expedition he’s with is looking for the missing link.’’

"Good," Sam said. He couldn't actually say he had liked Travis, but he hadn't wished the young man a bad life.

Al shook the handlink. The colors flared. Then he held it back up and shoved his unlit cigar in his mouth. "And that plan that he wanted Harding to back, the one with the sonar? A man named Adrian Shine did it in 1987. He must have been developing it while Travis was trying to get his father's help."

"Do you think Travis got the idea from him?"

"Who knows?" Al said, in a tone that implied Travis probably had. "Shine called the project Operation Deepscan. They had two dozen boats drop a sonar curtain over the lake and they swept it for three days."

"And came up dry," Sam said.

"No." Al stared at the handlink. "Near Urquhart Castle, they recorded something large moving slowly about six hundred feet below the surface."

"That's not very conclusive," Sam said.

"It is for me," Al said.

"Is that it?" Sam asked. "What about Sammi Jo? Does she come back to the Project?"

Al grinned. "Oh, yeah. She's here, Sam. She's working in a different division now, but she's one of our top theoretical physicists. She also has a specialty in artificial intelligence. She and Ziggy are working on ways to bring you back. And you know who she checks most of her theories with?"

Sam shook his head.

"Donald Harding. Seems this experience made quite an impression on him, and he's been a consultant to Project Quantum Leap from the start. He came to you, Sam, remember?"

Sam didn't remember, but it didn't matter. The time storm had ended. "I suppose he's still as charming as ever."

"We don't let him mingle with the staff much," Al said. "He never gets to do any public speaking, and I try to talk to him as little as possible."

"So if all is right with the world," Sam asked, "how come I haven't Leaped yet?"

"I don't know," Al said. "Maybe—you know—" he gestured upward—"is giving you some time with your daughter."

Sam grinned. He liked that idea. "If that's the case," he said, "I'd better go enjoy it."

"Be careful what you say!" Al said.

"I will," Sam said. He'd learned his lesson on that one. He'd be careful, but he'd get to know his adult daughter—as best he could in the time given him.

And maybe, just maybe, that would be enough.

CHAPTER TWENTY-SEVEN

When a distinguished but elderly scientist states that something is possible, he is almost certainly right. When he states that something is impossible, he is very probably wrong.

—ARTHUR C. CLARKE

Loch Ness, March 17, 1986.

"You know," Sam said. "It's Harding's turnaround that bothers me."

He was sitting on the dock, legs crossed, a fishing pole neglected by his side. The sun, weak and thin, and nearly gray, added a patina of silver on the loch. The water was usually still calm and flat. Al hovered over the water, unnerving Sam slightly. Sammi Jo and Travis were on the far side of the loch, taking photographs of things that existed—like the castle and the inn.

"He just doesn't strike me as the kind of guy who would change his mind so quickly."

Al shoved a hand in the gold pocket of his green and blue suit. Somehow he made the gaudy outfit look dapper. "That's my fault, Sam," Al said. "I brought him into the Project when we'd lost you, thinking he might be able to help."

Sam laughed. "So you broke the rules too."

Al shrugged. "It seemed right at the time."

"Yeah, I thought so too, but it nearly screwed us up." Sam looked across the loch. Sammi Jo was laughing, her head tilted back. These past two days had been incredibly precious to him. After Sammi Jo confronted Travis on the photos, and after Sam promised to have a more open mind—without the need for strong evidence—Travis had calmed down. Sammi Jo had suggested treating their visit to the inn as a real vacation, and for the last day and a half, the place had been filled with laughter.

Sam had missed that.

And he had needed it.

"I don't know if it screwed us up or not," Al said. "Ziggy thinks that you had to be here. That Harding couldn't have inspired anyone. The more I see of the guy, the more I'm sure Ziggy's right."

"You mean, I was supposed to inspire Sammi Jo?" Sam shook his head. "If that were the case, Al, I'd have Leaped by now."

"Maybe," Al said. "Maybe not."

Sam drew his coat around him. Despite the rare sunshine, the air was chill. "Still, you'd think—"

"S-S-Sam!" Al cried. He was staring beyond Sam and pointing with his cigar. "You'd better look at that!"

Sam followed the direction of Al's finger. In the center of the loch, a large thin neck rose. A diamond-shaped head crowned the top, with an eye as large as

Sam's fist, staring at him. Three more humps rose behind, and then a small, diamond-shaped tail.

It rose silently, with no splashes at all.

"Do you think it's the real thing?" Sam whispered.

"No, I think it's made of rubber. Of course it's real." Al had come closer to Sam. In fact Al was nowhere near the water now.

The monster's head turned. It looked like a brontosaurus, a small head on a powerful neck. Water dripped off its scales, and a clump of weeds clung to one hump.

It tilted its head so both eyes were visible.

"It sees you," Sam whispered.

"I know," Al said, "and it thinks I'm lunch! I'm getting out of here." He hit the handlink. The link squealed, but Al remained.

"Wait," Sam said. "How many times do you get to see a myth?"

"This is enough for me, thanks," Al said. He hit the link again.

"Travis!" Sam yelled. "Sammi Jo!"

The monster swam toward Al. Its head was covered with slime. The air smelled of stale lake water.

Sammi Jo and Travis had their backs to the creature. They were pointing at the castle.

"Sammi Jo!" Sam yelled again.

She didn't seem to hear him.

"I think he likes you, Sam," Al said, huddling close.

The monster was swimming rapidly toward the dock.

"If it's a he," Sam said. He wasn't sure he wanted to be this close. But a man couldn't get any more proof of impossible things than this. If that's what Harding needed, well, he had gotten it.

''Don't move,'' Al said.

''As if I could,'' Sam mumbled.

The monster opened its mouth—

And Sam Leaped.

About the Author

Sandy Schofield is the pen name for husband-and-wife writing team Dean Wesley Smith and Kristine Kathryn Rusch.

As Sandy Schofield, they have written three books: a *Star Trek: Deep Space Nine* novel called *The Big Game*, an *Aliens* novel called *Rogue*, and this novel.

Under their double byline, they have written several more *Star Trek* novels, including one part of last summer's smash hit, *The Invasion Series*. They also collaborated on a publishing company, Pulphouse Publishing, Inc. That joint venture has brought them one World Fantasy award, several other award nominations, and a house full of books (including several copies of *The Best of Pulphouse* from St. Martin's Press). Kristine edited *Pulphouse* for four years and *The Magazine of Fantasy and Science Fiction* for six years. Her work there won her science fiction's prestigious Hugo Award for Best Professional Editor. Dean edited most Pulphouse projects. His editing skills placed *Pulphouse: A Fiction Magazine* on the Hugo ballot four times.

Individually, Dean and Kristine have published shelves full of short stories and novels. Dean's novel, *Laying the Music to Rest*, was a finalist for the Bram Stoker Award for Best Horror Novel (the only science fiction novel to achieve that distinction). He has also sold over fifty short stories.

Kristine has sold a number of short stories as well as several novels. Her most recent novels are *The Fey: Rival* and *Star Wars: The New Rebellion*, both from Bantam Books. Dean and Kristine live in Oregon.